Gayle Siebert
Visit my website at www.gaylesiebert.com

# WEMBLY

—Gayle Siebert

Also by Gayle Siebert:

The Pillerton Secret
The Dark River Secret
Silver Buckles

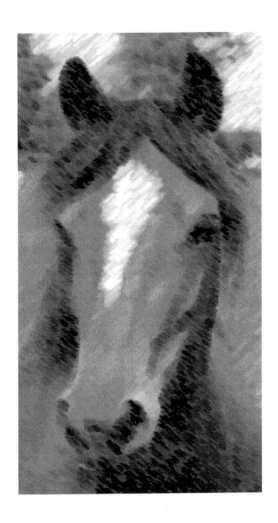

**Wembly,** by Lisa
Charcoal and chalk

# ONE

1

HAVE YOU EVER THOUGHT there are more Mondays than any of the other days in the week? More, say, than Saturdays or Sundays? It seems that way to me.

Every Monday right after dismissal I have to walk over to my brother Jemmy's school, nag at him while he fools around with his friends when he should be putting his jacket and boots on, and then we take the city bus to his karate class. When that noisy confusion's over, we walk to Dad's office and get a ride home with him. By then, being January, it's already dark.

I call him a big baby because he's afraid to go by himself. I say without me, he'd likely lose his bus pass and be stranded, or take the wrong bus and end up in Coombs. Or fall into a ditch somewhere. He gets all worked up and shouts: "I am not!" "I would not!" He never points out that it's not up to him; Mom and Dad don't want him going by himself. He's just a kid, eight years younger than me, so I guess I get it.

On the plus side, I get my homework done while I'm waiting at the dojo, and there are a couple of cute older karate guys to watch, too. You have to be careful, though; you don't want them to see you gawking or they'll think they're so special all they have to do is say one word to you and you'll be All Theirs. So I make sure and watch the little kids too. You know, I play it cool. Still, there's always a chance one of the cute guys will start up a conversation, and you never know what could happen from there.

Anyway. On this day, Jemmy already has his jacket and boots on. He's sitting on the bench all by himself, swinging his feet, waiting for me.

"Where's your friends?" I ask.

"Linden wouldn't let me play with him and Devon today."

It's on the tip of my tongue to say something like I told you to use mouthwash, but he looks so dejected I ruffle his hair and say, "Oh, I'm sorry. I guess you didn't have a very good day, then, did you?" He shakes his head while he studies his swinging feet.

It isn't unusual for that Linden kid to tell Jemmy he doesn't want to play with him. I wish Jemmy didn't like him so much. I wish Linden wasn't so mean. I wish

Linden would move to another school, or that Jemmy would make other friends and quit relying so much on Linden. But I'm afraid Jemmy will just keep getting his feelings hurt, and there's nothing I can do about it.

"Come on," I tell him, "let's get a move on or we'll miss the bus. Tell you what, I'll treat you to McDonalds after karate. We'll get Dad to meet us there."

He looks up and brightens a little. "Could I get a new Tech Deck?" He may only be seven, but he knows the McDonalds closest to the dojo is in Walmart, and if I'm in a treating mood, it's a good time to ask for more.

"I don't have enough money to go to McDonalds *and* get you a new Tech Deck, Jem. It's not allowance day for another week, you know. We'd have to skip McDonald's."

"We could skip McDonalds."

"Then what's the point of going to the mall?" I've got him there. To soften the blow, I remind him, "You know there's a toy in the kid's meal, right?"

He nods.

"Okay, then?"

"Okay."

"Where's your gi? Where's your back pack?"

"Oh! I forgot!" He jumps off the bench and runs back into his classroom. When he comes out, he's dragging his back pack and has a bundle of papers in his hand. These turn out to be his Works of Art. It looks like they've been stuffed in his cubby for a while. Possibly there was a PB and J in there with them at one time. He doesn't show promise as an artist, either. Despite the rumpled paper, greasy stains, and the fact I can't make out anything other than a stick man or two, I admire them; then he stuffs them in his backpack, and we set out.

If you think that was the end of the Tech Deck discussion, you can forget it. We're on the bus and Jemmy's been so quiet I've kind of forgotten about him, when he pipes up with: "When we go to McDonalds, you always just have fries, right?"

"Uh-huh," I say, wondering where this is going.

"If I just had fries instead of a Kid's Meal, would you have enough money for a Tech Deck then?"

He got me.

Of course, when we get home I still have barn chores to do, and it's a pain running the wheelbarrow out to the manure pile in the dark. Wembly makes up for it, though. He nickers when he sees me, tosses his head and does his little dance. He thinks I'm the Sun and the Moon. Maybe because I'm the Bringer of the Food.

4

## 2

WE LIVE IN SADDLE RIDGE, on a street called Saddle Ridge Way. It's a bunch of small acreages on the outskirts of the city. Most people living here keep horses, although at the end of the cul-de-sac, there's a Christmas tree farm with no horses. I call that a waste of a good pasture, especially when you can get a pre-decorated, pre-lit tree. After Christmas, five minutes and it's back in the box. No dead tree to haul to the chipper. No need to buy another tree next year. The only downside I can see is that you have to have a place to store the box. It's important to take care of the box! I can't stress this enough. Without the box, storage could be a problem. If you're thinking even storage of the box is a problem in your situation, say if you live in an apartment, I recommend you purchase a smaller tree, which of course, comes in a smaller box and will fit easily into even the smallest closet. So you see, artificial trees are way more sensible, and then that Christmas tree farm could be a nice field for horses.

If for some reason you don't want horses and you want to grow stuff you can sell, you should at least have trees that are good for something, like apples or walnuts, or bushes like blueberries. You know, to Feed the World. Plus, you can have a nice bunch of those trees and put horses in with them, like in our pasture, so it's multi-use. Just one of the things I've been thinking about lately.

Anyway. I got Wembly, my Quarter Horse gelding, six years ago, when I was almost ten and he was sixteen. He has a small barn that opens onto his field, so he can come and go when he wants to.

Dear sweet Wembly! So beautiful. So cute, with the crooked white stripe on his face. When his feet weren't sore, he carried me around the neighbourhood trails for hours on end. Even now, even with his sore feet, when he sees me coming from the school bus he whinnies like he hasn't seen me in a year and comes running to the fence.

I think Dad is hoping I'll lose interest in horses, because he's started mentioning that since Wembly isn't sound enough for me to do what I want to with him, he could go to the Therapeutic Riding Club so lots of kids could love him, or maybe I could find a home for him as a companion horse somewhere, and so on. I would never even consider moving him away from here! He may not be sound enough to do more than walk, although as I mentioned earlier he can run so long as it's his idea, but I still love him, and this is his home, after all. Besides, the people you give him to could do anything, even ship him, which is a horrible thing for a horse, but you have no control over that because he's not yours any more. I got Mom to promise he can live here until he dies. Dad doesn't argue with her.

It's true I would like to continue with taking riding lessons from the lady down the street, and Wembly can't do it. The obvious solution to that problem is to get another horse. They are herd animals after all, so Wembly would enjoy having company while he grows old and I'd have a horse to do all the stuff I used to do with Wembly. Dad gets a cranky look on his face when I bring up that subject and starts in about who's going to look after them when I go away to university, young ladies need to develop finesse, and so on. I'm still working on Mom. In her favour, she gives him a cranky look right back, and she has mentioned that if you have one horse, you might as well have two because you are tied down anyway. I don't like her calling it being "tied down" because that sounds too negative, but until I have a suggestion for a better-sounding phrase she could use, there you have it.

Anyway. Friday, I get off the bus and trot down the road toward our place. It's puzzling, but there's no Wembly whinnying and hinking along to greet me at the fence.

I put my backpack in the house and go straight up to the barn, thinking he's got himself locked in his stall. He's done that before. He fools around with the latch that holds the door open until it lets go, and then amuses himself swinging the door back and forth. If he happens to be inside the stall and it slams shut, he'll just stand there looking sheepish, waiting for me to come and open the door again. If it happens the hay net in the stall is empty, he manages to push the door open and free himself, though, so it's totally a con on his part. I make a big fuss like: "Oh poor Wembly, have you been locked in there all day?" and so on, letting him think he's pulled one over on me.

But today, there's no Wembly face hanging over the inside stall door. I go through his stall into his paddock and find him lying there, thrashing around in the mud. This is bad. I run to the house and call the veterinarian, then go back, put his halter on, and make him get up. He's sweating and keeps kicking at his belly.

I see Mom's car come in the driveway, and a short while later, Dad and Jemmy come home too. They're used to me being up at the barn with Wembly, so they don't come out. I didn't text Mom to tell her Wembly was sick, because I didn't want to worry her when she was at work, but I should've brought my phone with me so I could text her now. Anyway, when Doctor Bennie's truck drives in, Mom realizes there's a problem and joins me at the barn.

Doctor Bennie takes Wembly's temperature, then uses his stethoscope and listens to his heart, listens for gut sounds, and takes his pulse. He tells us Wembly's problem is colic, and he'll have to give him mineral oil.

He explains colic is caused by the intestines being blocked, either by an impaction or a twist in the intestine. If it's an impaction, the mineral oil should move things along. If not, there is no hope for Wembly other than surgery.

The surgery is expensive, and then Wembly will need five or six months of stall rest. About half the horses that have the surgery, Doctor Bennie says, colic again. He tells us about Big Ben, who had colic surgery twice and finally died of colic. Of course, Big Ben was a World Champion, didn't have sore feet, and was a lot younger than Wembly at least for the first two surgeries. He says even though Wembly isn't a World Champion, his life is just as important as Big Ben's but surgery isn't a cure, and it's not always the kindest thing to do.

He threads a length of rubber tubing through Wembly's nostril into his stomach and pours in a whole jug of mineral oil. He puts on a surgical glove that reaches all the way up to his shoulder and slides his hand and arm as far into Wembly's colon as he can. At last, he gives him an injection, which seems to make him better.

"He's feeling better now, Lisa, but it's only because of the shot I gave him. This isn't a cure," he says. "It might wear off. I'm going to go and do a few things, but I'll check back with you in a couple of hours. If his symptoms return, I'll come back."

Before he leaves, he tells us to keep Wembly walking around, although he can just stand, too, as long as he doesn't lie down again, because once he's down it might not be possible to stop him from rolling, and that's very bad.

Mom says she'll walk Wembly while I go in the house and eat my dinner, but I don't think I'll be able to swallow a thing, I'm so worried about Wembly, even though he looks fine now. I keep hoping he'll poop, but he doesn't; in a few hours, he's sweating and kicking at his belly again. Mom calls Doctor Bennie.

Doctor Bennie comes back and checks Wembly over like he did before. His face looks grim. We talk about the surgical option. Mom says she would pay for the surgery, but I should think of Wembly. Six months of stall rest? And this might happen again? On top of it all, his sore front feet flare up more often and he's in pain a lot of the time. I've been giving him pain medication, but it seems to be less and less effective.

As much as I wish otherwise, surgery isn't in the cards for Wembly. All I can do is hope he'll get through this without it, which seems more and more unlikely since the mineral oil hasn't moved anything along.

Mom and I take turns leading Wembly around the little pond of light from the barn door to make sure he doesn't lie down and roll. Big Mutt, our Heinz 57 black and tan dog, follows for a while before giving up and just sitting on the concrete pad in front of the door, in the way, as usual.

Dad comes out and watches for a few minutes. Then he tells Doctor Bennie to come into the house to warm up and have a coffee and whenever he feels like it, and leaves. He's not fond of being in the barn at the best of times.

The hours pass slowly. Mom and I walk Wembly around and around, always hoping he will poop. Drink. At least want to graze. He doesn't.

Finally, around six a.m., Doctor Bennie checks him again. My insides all clench as he turns to me, shakes his head and says, "Still no sounds in his cecum."

I can see Wembly is in agony; his lips are pressed together, and his eyes look dull. I realize we're not going to get him through and the right thing to do is to euthanize him.

As the sky lightens in the pre-dawn, I lead him to a rise in his field by the apple tree where he likes to stand when he naps. I bring the dream catcher I made at camp the summer I got him and clip it onto his halter. His name is glued on it in glitter letters. I want him to have it with him when he gets to the Rainbow Bridge. I hope it will guarantee him safe passage. You know, introduce him and prove someone loved him very much and that he was a good boy all his life. I can't help it, I'm crying.

As if to tell me it's okay, Wembly gives my hand a little nudge with his big lip. I start yodeling like never before. Mom ties one of her beautiful silk scarves around his neck and then draws me into a hug.

Doctor Bennie administers the lethal drug. Wembly falls with a resounding **whump!** and never moves again.

CR80CR

I should explain my thoughts about the Rainbow Bridge. I'm looking at the world and my life differently lately, questioning a lot of things. I don't know if there is such a thing as a Rainbow Bridge, but if there's any chance there is, I want Wembly to have safe passage.

And somehow, thinking about Wembly crossing it with that old dreamcatcher and Mom's scarf is a comfort.

# 3

LATER THAT MORNING, a backhoe comes and digs a grave. I just can't bring myself to go out and watch as he's buried; instead, I retreat to my bedroom but can't stop imagining sweet, beautiful Wembly with his dreamcatcher and Mom's scarf being pushed into the hole and covered with dirt. I might have been better off going to watch.

Mom scissored off Wembly's forelock; she gives it to me so I can braid it and have that to remember him by. She hugs me a whole bunch and says the hurt will go away. Then she offers to make a hair appointment, maybe I'd like to have some highlights done? Or we can shop for new clothes. As if I'm interested in either of those things.

Jemmy only knows that the horse doctor came, Wembly is buried and his big sister is sad. He and Big Mutt come and snuggle in beside me on my bed. Well, if you can call what Jemmy does snuggling. He runs his new Tech Deck along the top of the headboard so many times I wonder how he doesn't get tired of it, spins his Fidget Spinner until I wish it would quit Spinning, Fidget or otherwise, and generally makes constant noise. Normally I'd tell him he sounds like he belongs in the monkey house at the zoo and that he doesn't have to be making noises all the time, but today I don't natter at him about it because I'm touched that he's trying to make me feel better. Still, if you think I beg him to stay when he says he's going across the road to Devon's house, you can forget it.

After I mope around for a day or two, I start wanting someone to talk to. Someone who understands. The only one I can think of is Nicole. Once, we were inseparable. Nicole sold her pony, Jackson, a couple of years ago. Despite the hours we'd spent talking about how she'd get a Quarter Horse like Wembly when she outgrew Jackson, Jackson went but no bigger horse came. Even just last fall we always ate lunch together, but now Nicole has new friends and hardly ever eats lunch with me. We don't have much to talk about any more because now she's not interested in anything but boys and going to the mall and there's only so much of that I can stand.

But the biggest thing, the worst thing, is that she's no fun any more. She used to be funny. We laughed a lot. But now she's all serious or what she calls acting like a grown up, and doesn't think I'm funny, either. For example, the Stew Incident. She was having the Tuesday Special, which was a little pot of stew with a biscuit. I didn't have stew, for two reasons:

one, I'm questioning the morality of slaughtering animals, so I want to be a vegan or maybe only a pescatarian because I'm not quite ready to give up tuna; and two, that gray gloop they called stew looked suspicious to me, and I told Nicole that. As she was poking her fork around in it to see what it might be that I didn't like the looks of, I came out with:

> There was a young man from Peru
> Who found a large mouse in his stew
> Said the waiter, don't shout
> And wave it about,
> Or the rest will be wanting one, too.

She told me to grow up. See? She not only didn't think it was funny, but she doesn't even appreciate poetry. It would be childish to stick my tongue out at her even though it was definitely a tongue-sticking-out moment, so I hung my spoon on my nose instead. If you've tried it, you know it's harder than it looks. From the look she gave me, I'm pretty sure she can't do it.

Anyway. You can see we've grown apart, but still, I think Nicole will understand. She comes. She tears up a bit and then reminds me Jackson is gone although he didn't die, she says she doesn't even miss him, and she bets that pretty soon I won't miss Wembly, either. Her saying that hurts, but I try to take it in the spirit it was meant, like, to be a comfort.

We start listening to music on her iPhone, talking about school, moaning about algebra. She gives herself a good long look in the mirror over my dresser as she fusses with her hair. "Didn't you notice my hair? I had it done yesterday. Isn't this colour great?" she asks.

Her hair is naturally blonde, but now it's brown. I was shocked when I saw it, I just didn't say anything, and if you think I'm dumb enough to tell her I think it's awful because it's too dark for her complexion, you can forget it. I say I think her natural colour is beautiful and most people myself included would kill for it, and anyone can have brown hair, in my opinion. I thought it was a compliment but going by the look she gives me, she doesn't take it that way. Good thing I didn't say what I really thought! I guess she just wanted me to agree with her. To her credit, she doesn't tell me I'm nobody's go-to person for fashion advice since my Mom still buys most of my clothes. I wish I hadn't told her that.

Anyway. She lets it pass and starts babbling about the hot new boy in her history class (he's not very tall but lucky for her, she's not as tall as I am so she can still wear heels they will make a cute couple) and so on.

I can get a never get a word in when she starts running off at the mouth like this, which is okay, because I'm busy trying to figure out who it is she's talking about. I've noticed some new faces, but I don't remember seeing anyone so off-the-charts good looking in the whole school.

Then she's going on about how badly she wants a dress she's seen at The Gap. She really *really* needs it for the Valentine's dance. She's almost got her parents convinced she needs her own credit card, and if they give it to her, she'll be able to buy it! Maybe this weekend! She hopes hopes *hopes* the new guy will ask her and she *guarantees* he'll be *blown away* when he sees her in it! And I shouldn't worry because if he doesn't ask her to go to the dance with him, there's this other guy on the basketball team she kind of likes and he's super tall so tall even I could wear heels if I went out with him which won't happen because he's older and doesn't go for girls like me.

"Girls like me?"

"Oh, you know, he likes girls with The Look."

I nod as if I know what she's talking about. I do remember her telling me a few years ago that I couldn't be an airline stewardess because I don't have The Look. I was only halfway interested in being a sky waitress anyway. She has The Look I guess, because she'll be going to the dance with one of those guys, for sure, and do I think she should get burgundy or purple streaks in her hair? I already told her what I thought of her hair, so I'm not surprised she doesn't wait for me to answer.

"I'll show you the dress I'm talking about. There's one like it online!" She looks around my room. "Where's your computer?"

"You know I don't have my own. Our family computer's downstairs."

"Seriously? FFS, you *still* don't have your own? How do you Snapchat or Facebook with your parents hanging over your shoulder? Do you just use your phone?"

"Sure, I use my phone for Facebook. But I'm not on very much. Anyway, why would I care if my parents see what I'm doing?" I ask. "It's not like I'm stupid enough to post naked pictures."

Nicole frowns, clamps her lips together into a hard line, and says, "It's like you're in the dark ages, FFS! You need to get on Snapchat. Instagram, too. And everyone has a laptop! I can't believe you!" She clicks her tongue, sort of strides around the bed a couple of times, then says, "Never mind. I took a picture. You won't get the full effect on this small screen, though." She gets busy on her phone.

"Besides," I continue, picking up where I left off and ignoring her opinion regarding my lack of a laptop and my failings social media-wise, "I hardly ever look at Facebook, like I said. Too much of a time suck. I'm busy with school work, and Wembly ..." catching myself, I turn away and sink to my bed. With my face in the pillow, I start yodeling like a Swiss mountain climber. I keep it up until I have a pounding headache.

"Sorry, Nicole!" I say when I've mostly quit blubbering, "I thought I was all cried out, but I just c-can't stop hearing the sound of h-him hitting the g-ground!"

Nicole doesn't say anything, not that I know of anyway, because she's gone. I guess I can't blame her. I wouldn't want to sit and watch someone all ugly-faced with crying just because of a soon-to-be-forgotten horse, either.

ೞఐೞ

My parents conclude I've moped around the house long enough and tell me it's time I went back to school. It will help get my mind off it, Mom says. Dad chooses this moment to point out the barn will make a great shed to park the new ride-on mower he'll get as now there will be even more grass to mow. Mom gives him a dark look. He ignores it.

I think he's really looking forward to that new mower. He doesn't seem to realize the reason he needs it for all that extra grass is what causes the awful squeezing feeling in my chest.

# TWO

1

I HUNCH DOWN over the water fountain. I'm as close
to the wall as possible, because you know how big your
butt looks when you bend over like that and I definitely
don't want mine sticking out into the hall. Not that
there's anyone around to see it, but you never know
when someone might come along, you know, just
quietly strolling along until BOOM! Right behind you,
with a fine view of your ass. So I make it a habit not to
have it sticking out into the hall.

I've already taken four or five drinks in the past
half hour, so I'm not thirsty; it's just part of my cover. I
admit it's what Mom would call a thin excuse for being
here. People with lockers along this hall left at least an
hour ago, and my locker is two flights up and at the
other end of the school. The real reason I'm here is that
this water fountain is right outside the boy's locker

room. Basketball practice must be over by now. What's keeping Jarrett?

I shift my backpack from my right shoulder to my left, then set it down. It's heavy. I need to empty some stuff out of it, but the only time I think of it is when I'm packing it around. Once I'm home, you can forget it, there are too many other things on my mind.

The door crashes open. Finally! Raucous boy-man voices and clouds of Christmas-gift cologne pour into the hallway with the basketball players. They all have shower wet hair. I quickly bend over the fountain again, facing their way of course, and then straighten up. Hopefully the expression on my face makes me look surprised rather than stunned. It's a tough expression to get right. I've been practicing, but it's still hit and miss.

"Hey, Munroe!"—Ethan, the team captain laughs— "Here she is again! Maybe you should keep your pets at home." He grabs Jarrett's arm, and shoves him into me.

"Yeah, Munroe!" Tall Tyler Robinson pushes his lanky frame between Jarrett and me, and with one of his ape arms around each of us, pulls us rudely together. I get a whiff of Jarrett's breath. He must have had Caesar salad or something else with a lot of garlic in it for dinner last night. If it wasn't for his friends being here, I'd say *Ewww! Hell-a-TOSIS!* which has been a joke between us since we learned the word back when we were about ten and we each accused the other of having it even if it wasn't true. I squirm to try and get away. I can feel my face turning red.

Tyler wouldn't be Tyler if he didn't have something he thinks is hilarious to say. He screws up his face. "Whew! What's that smell? Perfume? Oh, yeah, I think I recognize it now—Eau de Stable, isn't it?"

"Back off, Ty!" Jarrett gives Tyler a shove that sends him stumbling into the boys behind him. Everyone laughs. Everyone but Jarrett and me, that is. Jarrett is turning red, too, probably just as red as me. His eyes are going black and his forehead creases in a frown that causes his eyebrows to nearly join up. I know that look! Time to back slowly away.

Tyler must have seen the look before, too, because he stays back. Making fanning motions in front of this face with a long hand, he says: "Too much for me, man. Hey! Any you guys know the difference between a horse girl and a farmer? Well, farmers have the shit on the outside of their boots."

The boys all hoot and holler like it's the funniest thing they've heard in their lives. I don't know, maybe they're imagining horse manure squishing up between my toes, which is ridiculous. Horse manure isn't that squishy, as a rule.

Anyway. They sweep away down the hall, shoes squeaking on the floor as they push and shove each other like a bunch of young bulls. You can see why it's mostly boys who play football. Laughter fades as their red and gold team jackets round the corner into the main corridor, leaving Jarrett and me alone at the water fountain.

My cheeks feel as if they're on fire and I can't look Jarrett in the eye. It's not wise to make eye contact with him when he's got that look anyway. You wouldn't stare at an angry dog, would you? Instead, I study what I can see of the cowboy boots I got for Christmas sticking out under the hem of my jeans. They're perfectly clean inside *and* out and have multi-coloured embroidered flowers spilling across the toes. They are every bit as cute as the Mandela boots Nicole is all giddy about, in my opinion.

I take a deep breath, push Tyler Robinson's remarks out of my mind, and steal a look at Jarrett's face. The black look is mostly gone. Even so, I have to be careful how I start. You always have to be careful how you start talking to Jarrett or he'll dive in before you're half done and start off in another direction and you won't get a chance to finish your thought. So you have to make your point real quick.

I've been rehearsing what I would say, but now there's a lump in my throat. I swallow a couple of times.

"It's just"—I begin— "that is, what I was calling you about—"

"Lisa," Jarrett cuts me off, "you gotta quit this! You're embarrassing me. And I won't stand up for you again. I mean it!"

Then his expression softens. He cups my shoulders and squeezes gently. "Look, Lisa. Laurie Ann was pissed because you were hanging around my locker. Do you think I'll hang with you when Laurie Ann is right there?"

"But I just—"

"And you keep calling me! She sees your picture pop up on my phone, so I can't answer. I keep telling her we're just friends, but she doesn't believe it. She says I have to decide if I want a *girlfriend*, or a *girl friend*. Understand?"

I don't, really. He can't even talk to me on the phone without his new girlfriend getting her panties in a bunch? He's had plenty of time to call me when she's not around, too. He'd be better off with me as a friend than her as a girlfriend, in my opinion, but if you think

I'm going to tell him that, you can forget it! In fact, I don't get a chance to say anything at all before he drops his hands and hurries after the other boys.

I slump back against the wall. "He liked Wembly," I say to no one. I guess I'll have to tell him in a text that Wembly died, although that seems harsh. Maybe I won't tell him. Maybe he doesn't care anyway. Maybe I'll just put it on Facebook.

I swallow some more and try to choke down the painful lump in my throat. I still can't get through an hour without reliving that awful night, that awful final thump. I scrunch my eyes shut but tears well up and trickle down my cheeks anyway. I rub them off on my sleeve.

I push away from the wall, hoist my backpack over my shoulder, and walk to the exit, through the doors, and out into the grey January. It's raining. More than just drizzle. Dropping my backpack on a planter, I pull out my hoodie and vest, slip them on, and bring the hood over my head. The vest is waterproof, but the hoodie isn't. I'll be soaked by the time I get home.

A car screams out of the parking lot, fishtailing on the wet pavement as it turns, then straightens, and speeds past. It's Ethan's car, and he's at the wheel. There's another boy in front; Jarrett's in the back. A fluffy blonde head huddles next to him. I don't have to see her face to know it's Laurie Ann.

Laurie Ann Reedy. The most popular girl in school. Everyone says she should be dating the most popular boy, Ethan Carter, not Jarrett Munroe, who isn't even in the "in" crowd. Or at least wasn't, until he started dating Laurie Ann.

I have to give Laurie Ann credit. Jarrett is better looking than Ethan, so he would be the obvious choice, halitosis aside, and in fairness he doesn't always have it. So I can't blame her for snatching him up. Would he still be "in" with the popular kids if he chose me over Laurie Ann? Probably not. As much as I'd like to, I can't blame Jarrett.

"Bet she won't tell him he has halitosis!" I say to no one. I would call him on it every time, and honesty being important, that makes me the better person, in my opinion.

I'm glad there aren't any other kids around, though, because they'd think I was having an episode, standing out in the rain muttering to myself.

Hoisting my backpack, I start off. The raindrops cooling my face are welcome. It's a long walk home. I'm glad of that. I'm not in a hurry. Nothing to hurry home for any more. The thought of Wembly not being there to greet me raises that lump in my throat again; I can't stop myself this time, and I start yodeling away. Luckily, I'm alone on the sidewalk, so I turn my face up to the sky and let the tears run down my face, mixing with the rain.

The rain is drenching my head and the sleeves of my hoodie, too. I'm getting cold, and I wish I'd taken the bus after all. If I had, that whole unpleasant scene with Jarrett wouldn't have happened.

A car slows as it comes up beside me, then stops at the curb ahead as if waiting for me. Even from behind I recognize Tyler Robinson's extra-large ears. The passenger window glides open as I catch up. He leans across the seat and calls out, "Hey, Lisa! Like my new ride? Hop in! I'll give you a lift."

As if! I'd have to be a lot colder to get in the car with him! I keep walking.

He drives forward slowly to keep pace with me. "Come on! You're getting soaked!"

"Wouldn't want to stink up your car, Robinson!" I tell him. My voice doesn't sound as firm as I'd like, being a bit quavery from that yodeling I mentioned.

"Hey, I was just kidding about that! Sorry if it hurt your feelings. I'll make it up to you. Buy you a Coke?"

He leans across and pushes the passenger side door open.

The easement that leads to the paved path paralleling the Parkway is just a few meters ahead. I start into a jog and turn down it.

# 2

NEXT MORNING, I'm at my locker stashing my backpack and getting the books I need for the morning's classes, when suddenly Tyler is standing over me.

"Hey, Lisa!" he says, grinning and flicking my braid.

I put up my arm, hand toward him. Where is that crucifix or holy water. Pepper spray. Stun gun. Stock prod. At least a bunch of garlic. When you need it?

"Cat got your tongue?" he persists. I'm tall, but he's one of the tallest boys in school, and hovers over me. Coach Baker's reasons for wanting him on the team are obvious, although I wonder how he can run without tripping over those big feet. But then, besides being tall, his hands are so long he can hold a basketball with just one, and I mean upside down, you know, with his hand on top. That's got to be a big advantage.

"Seriously," Tyler says, still with that toothy grin, "look! I brought you something—a gift—to say sorry for yesterday." He pulls his hand halfway out of the pocket of his team jacket and turns it palm up, displaying a small Ziploc bag with a few pills inside. They might be aspirins but for the colour and the "Z" stamped on them.

"Let's go have some fun," he says in a loud whisper, leaning even closer.

I back away as far as I can, but with my locker door in the way, I end up just pressing into my locker.

"Are you nuts?" I ask, and turn so he's behind me. I get a sinking feeling when I realize I just rubbed my butt against him. "Go away!" I tell him. I'm so embarrassed, my voice is louder than I meant it to be, and I see some of the other kids in the hall are gawking.

Tyler is behind me for a few more seconds before he turns and joins the lava flow of moving students, a head taller than the rest. I wonder why there's a cocky bounce in his step when he's just been told off.

And what about the amused chuckles from other kids in the hall? Jarrett or someone must have told Laurie Ann about what happened yesterday and she's likely been blabbing about it. Her locker is across the hall from mine, and she's there now, surrounded by her friends. She draws them close and says something, setting off a chorus of giggles. They look at me and giggle some more. I organize my books, close my locker, then turn my back on Laurie Ann and her sycophants and walk away, striding along as if I've got an important destination in mind.

I should mention here that I don't always think of that group as "Laurie Ann and her sycophants". That's too cumbersome, even though *sycophants* is a neat word, but except for Laurie Ann and Emily, I don't know their names. I've given them all Temporary Names: Broom-Hilda, Magica, Haggedy and Zelda, plus few others. These are just the four flocking around her now. If you think these sound like names of witches, High Five to you! And you'll understand why I call them The Coven.

Anyway. I only take half a dozen steps away from The Coven before I realize my first class is the at the other end of the school and I'm going the wrong way. I'm not going to give them more giggle material by pulling a U-turn like I have no clue where I am or where I'm supposed to be, so I duck into the girls' washroom. They're gone when I come out again.

# 3

I HAVE CLASSES WITH some of those girls and even
Laurie Ann but manage to ignore them. At noon, I can't
find Nicole. I look in the lunch room. Laurie Ann and
The Coven are there. Zelda looks up, says something to
the others, and points at me. They all turn to look at me
and the tittering starts up again.

I should explain why I call Laurie Ann's friend
Zelda. She doesn't look like Princess Zelda in the
games if that's what you're thinking. She has squinty
eyes and kind of a pointy nose, and long black hair, so I
really should have named her after one of the witches.
But Zelda seems like a better name for a witch than for
a princess, and it's my story, after all. She's not in any
of my classes and there's no chance Laurie Ann will
introduce me, so she'll be Zelda in my mind probably
forever. Maybe it's not nice, but don't worry, I'd never
call her that to her face. At least I probably wouldn't.

I don't see any friendly faces, so I leave. I go
outside and head for the parking lot as if I'm going to
eat lunch with someone in their car. Of course, I'm not.
I walk around the block eating my sandwich as I go.

Okay, I know that's pathetic. I don't know
anyone with a car. Well, except as I already mentioned,
Tyler Robinson, but I'd bungy jump naked before I'd

get in his car. That's saying a lot because the thought of bungy jumping even fully clothed makes my heart pound, and not in a good way.

After last class, I avoid more finger-pointing and giggling from The Coven by not going to my locker. Instead, I go to the library and sit with the losers serving detentions, ignore their whispering and spit balling, and do my Socials and Algebra homework.

When detentions are over, the librarian shoos us out. The school is quiet, and the halls are empty except for me and the kids that were in detention. I'm the only one going up to the second floor. I stow my books in my locker and pull out my backpack. My text message alert sounds; I get my phone out of my pocket, and see the message is from Mom. Who else? She wants me to start dinner.

When I get back down to the main entrance, I see the book sale volunteers were busy this afternoon. There are rows of tables topped with cardboard boxes everywhere.

Art classes have been working all week on posters for the literacy project book sale Friday. There's a big one depicting what could either be puke or chocolate chip cookies; I'm going to go with cookies. The lettering isn't bad, though, and despite possible confusion about the cookie/puke thing, it gets the point across: The Home Ec classes have been baking cookies all week and you should Bring Your Cookie Money Friday!

I see the poster I made pinned to the cork board nearest the auditorium doors in what I'd like to say is a position of prominence owing to its excellence, and next to it, one written in freehand with a wide chisel-point black felt reminding everyone donations of books are still needed and can be left in the boxes. Not even a sketch of some books? At least a smiley face?

I'm considering getting a felt out of my backpack and jazzing the sign up a bit when I hear what sounds like jabbering monkeys, and half the basketball team floods the foyer. I didn't think there would be practice two days in a row! Still, the buses must have left over an hour ago, and I know some of those guys have cars, so why are they going out the front door when the door nearest the gym goes straight out into the parking lot? Sometimes what boys do defies logic, proving what I've suspected for a long time, they're just not as smart as girls.

The entrance foyer would normally be plenty big enough for all of us to mill around there no problem, but with the tables set up for the book sale, there's only a narrow aisle down the middle. Trapped, I bolt for the door ahead of them, even though I'd rather not have them behind me. You know the old question, do these jeans make my ass look fat? I'm pretty skinny, but I still worry about it, ever since about three years ago when Jarrett commented on it. That was when we spent a lot of time together, before his family moved away.

"Hey, Lisa!" one of the boys whose voice I don't recognize calls out, "Come with us why doncha? We'll have a *real* good time!" They all hoot as if it's hilarious.

I think about stopping to let them pass but decide against it in case they think I'm waiting to talk to that jerk off. Jarrett could have said something, but he must be laughing along with the others. I guess he meant it when he said he wouldn't stand up for me again. He's one of them now, a member of The Team.

I walk faster. Once through the door, I jog down the steps and onto the sidewalk. I keep my head down and I'm soon out of earshot. It's another long walk home in steady January drizzle. I zip up my jacket. There are a couple of good things: one, I have my waterproof jacket today; and two, walking will give me plenty of time to think.

I know this stupid stuff with Jarrett will end. It was nothing anyway, despite what those morons seem to think. By next week, it'll be old news. Tomorrow, I'll eat lunch in the lunchroom, whether I know anyone there or not. I managed to ignore the basketball team and The Coven in class today and I can ignore them in the lunch room too. Besides, there are other girls I know, Angie Clark for one. Her locker is right beside mine. Maybe we'll have lunch together.

Still, Nicole's been my friend since we were little kids, and I miss her. But now she hangs with the girls who like what she likes: shopping, parties, boys, and maybe drugs? Although I don't know about the drugs. I don't think she's totally a member of The Coven yet, so maybe she can still be my friend, too. If I can make myself more like her, except for the not liking horses any more part, and not the drug part if she does drugs which as I mentioned, I don't know, maybe she and Jarrett both can still be my friends.

Where to start? Should I just copy how Nicole dresses, wears her hair, talks, and giggles? Well, not the giggling. I'm no good at that. Not that I don't have a sense of humour; I do, it's just that giggling over anything and everything is beyond annoying and my eyes just naturally roll up in my head. Probably not in my favour if I want Nicole to still be my friend. I'll make a point of looking at her shoes when she giggles. She does have a lot of cute shoes.

When I think about it, if I was really a friend, I guess I would have paid more attention to the songs she wanted me to listen to. And what about the boys she thinks are so hot? I didn't even ask their names. But right then I couldn't think of anything but Wembly. Songs, dresses, boys, it's all frivolous, in my opinion. I suppose she feels the same way about horses. But if I want to fit in, I'll need to be less judgmental.

I'm not like Nicole, though; I miss Wembly and I still love horses and want horses in my life. I'm not like Laurie Ann or any of the other popular girls, either. I don't fit in the way I am. The best I can do is to try and combine liking horses with being more like them. I'll dress like they do and when they're around, I won't mention horses. Tomorrow, I'll start a conversation with Nicole. It'll be easy; all I have to do is ask if either boy has asked her to the dance. I'll get her to describe that dress, and maybe I can even throw in a giggle or two. In minutes she'll be yammering away for the rest of the lunch hour. Yammering? Way to be less judgmental, Lisa!

# 4

AT HOME, I GET A TEXT from Mom saying she'll pick up Chinese, so I don't need to get dinner started after all. Since I have this unexpected luxury of free time and no parental supervision, I go into the master ensuite bathroom and try on lipstick. On Mom, it looks nice; on me, every shade just makes me look like my lips could enter a room minutes ahead of the rest of me. I look like Ronald McDonald, especially since there are two more areas of resemblance: one, my red hair; and two, next to Nicole's size fives, my shoes look like clown shoes. If I was going to Temporary-Name me, I'd call myself Ronald. I give it up and go to my room.

Although I don't have lipstick, I do have the rest of what Dad calls war paint, in a bin on my dresser. He goes on about how a little make-up is nice, but I should keep in mind there's a tipping point between tasteful make-up and war paint, in his opinion. He must have noticed I hardly ever wear makeup, so I don't know why he's worried. Just in case I start, maybe.

He must think Mom's not on top of my personal development, or that it's important to have a man's opinion. Besides warning me not to wear too much make-up, Dad is fond of explaining how every young lady needs to acquire finesse. He has plenty of suggestions for how I should go about acquiring finesse, largely centering around less barn/horse; university education; domestic skills, and so forth. His main objection to the barn/horse thing seems to be my constantly dirty fingernails. So far, although I try and remember to clean my nails often, I disappoint him in the finesse department. Maybe black nail polish is the way to go.

Anyway. I dig the tube of foundation out of the bin, open it, and looking in the dresser mirror, dab some across my cheeks like they show you on YouTube. When I blend it in it mostly covers my freckles and I'm pretty happy with that. With mascara and eye shadow to top it off, I'm practically made over. As I mentioned, I almost never bothered with make-up before, because ... Well, you know. Wembly. I'll have plenty of time to spend getting ready for school now that I have no morning barn chores.

I lie face down on my bed and cradle my head in the pillow. It just hit me again: Wembly's gone. How long will it take before thoughts of him stop ambushing me? At least this time, my yodeling only lasts a minute or two. I wonder if the streaks of eye shadow and mascara I just left on my pillow will come out in the wash.

I take a deep breath. I need something to do to get my mind off the fact that on a normal day I'd be out in the barn with Wembly. Now having free time because of not having to start dinner doesn't seem like such a gift. But it does mean I have plenty of time go on Facebook and see what Nicole's been posting lately. I open Facebook on my phone and go to her page. You wouldn't believe how many selfies she posts! I bet there's at least one every day.

I look at about a hundred photos of Nicole in various poses: mirror images, from the top down, hunched over, hair covering half her face, hair in a pony tail, red lips black lips white lips, in ripped-up jeans, in shorts, in leggings, in a bikini, in a bikini top and leggings, in chairs with one leg up, upside down on the couch with both legs over the back, and so on. She sure is talented at taking selfies.

I go through my clothes in hopes of putting together a Nicole-esque outfit. Obviously, the bikini ensembles are out, but I try on almost everything and end up with a pile of clothes I've outgrown. There isn't much left. Maybe I need to do some shopping after all. I'll ask Nicole if she'll go with me and help me pick out a few things. That way, I'll be sure of choosing the right stuff.

For now, there's a pair of skinny jeans with just a few little rips I got the last time I went shopping with Nicole, which was before school started last year. I hardly ever wear them because they're so low rise that when I sit, it feels like they're going to slide off my butt and I worry someone sitting behind me might get a view of something I'd rather they didn't. I'm not a plumber after all. Besides, cold air comes in through those rips I mentioned. At least I know they meet Nicole's approval, and I have a top that's close to what Nicole wears. I put these aside to put on in the morning.

The top is pretty, if a little revealing. It won't look the same on me as it would on Nicole, though. On her, you'd be able to see cleavage behind the lace peek-a-boo section, because her boobs are a little bigger than mine. Okay, a lot bigger. She's had boobs since Grade Seven. Mom says she was an Early Bloomer, and that I shouldn't worry, I'm just a Late Bloomer, and I'll get mine soon enough. *Not* soon enough, in my opinion. On the upside, I imagine boobs get in the way when you're shooting pool. Maybe that's something I should take it up.

Besides having bigger boobs, Nicole is curvier everywhere, and although Jarrett never said anything about *her* butt, she's definitely curvier there too. She quit growing up and started growing out, while I kept growing up. Anyway, the T-shirt is cute, and with the makeup, it's a start. It might even be a New Lisa Look I can be comfortable with. Having a plan makes me feel better.

I lie on my bed, close my eyes, and let mental images of Wembly slide show through my mind. I don't allow my brain to instant replay the awful final thump. Why do these happy memories make me feel so sad?

CR80CR

# THREE

## 1

IS IT MY IMAGINATION, or did Zelda deliberately hip check me into the lockers just now? Zelda is a big girl, and quite sturdy; it hurt my shoulder, but I don't let on. It must have been an accident. She did say sorry, even if she said it really loud and the other girls giggled. I'd been in a world of my own, rehearsing what to say when I caught up with Nicole in the lunchroom. I was probably not paying attention to where I was going.

I merge with the queue going into the cafeteria, pick up a tray and slide it along. I've decided to get a bowl of soup to go with my sandwich, and while I'm stuck waiting for the line to move, I scan the tables for Nicole. I didn't manage to meet up with her at her locker either before class or lunch, but I know she's at school today, because I spotted her in the lava flow of students changing classes earlier. She looked back and I waved, but she kept going. I guess she didn't see me.

I get to the soup pots, fill a bowl with vegetarian vegetable, grab a pack of saltines, and pay. When I walk toward the tables, I see Nicole with a couple of other girls. I know them, too, in the way everyone knows everyone in their grade at least, even though I've never met them. I don't think they're in The Coven, so that's promising in two ways: one, if Nicole's with them instead of with The Coven, she's not a hundred percent one of them yet; and two, I feel like it's okay to join them. I haven't seen them often enough to name them, though, which is just as well because once, the name I gave someone came out accidentally when I finally met her. Back then, she had shoulder-length, wavy blondish hair and big, brown, puppy-dog eyes that reminded me of Fido, the Cocker Spaniel we had when I was little. I loved that dog, so really, it was a compliment.

I go to Nicole's table. "Hi Nicole," I say as I put my tray on the table next to her, pull out the chair, and sit. I make eye contact with each of the girls across the table. "I think we're in some of the same classes. I'm Lisa."

Nicole grunts what might be hello but doesn't introduce the other girls and they don't tell me their names. Instead, they snicker, rise, and leave, dumping their trays on the clean-up counter as they go out.

I'm stunned and can't think of anything to say. "Is it my breath?" is all I can come up with.

Nicole says nothing. This isn't like her. It might be harder than I thought to draw her into a conversation. But I summon the ideas I came up with yesterday and rehearsed on my way in, and push on. "I was wondering," I say as I smash the crackers in their little cello package before sprinkling them on my soup, "about that new guy in your Socials class..."

"What about him?"

"Has he asked you to the dance yet? Or the basketball player?"

Nicole still says nothing. Instead she picks up her phone, scrolls through it, and shows me a photo of a person. Well, only the person's torso, the bottom of her chin and jaw. But you might not notice the chin and jaw, since the torso is naked and staring right out at you are boobs.

"You don't post naked pictures of yourself, but you don't mind sending this to Jarrett?"

"What?!?"

"Don't play dumb. Everyone's seen it."

"But that's ridiculous! I would never do that! Nicole, you know I would never do that! And you *know* that's not me! Let's go talk to Jarrett—"

"As if!" She snorts and stands abruptly, scraping the chair back noisily as she does. "Haven't you figured out Jarrett is Laurie Ann's boyfriend now? You better leave him alone if you know what's good for you! And you better quit stalking the basketball team!" She picks up her tray and charges away.

My stomach squeezes shut. I can't draw a full breath. I feel my pulse pounding. It's nauseating. Dizzying. *Everyone's* seen it? *Everyone* thinks that's me and I sexted Jarrett? Suddenly I know the reason for the stares, chuckles and giggles that have been following me.

When I feel able to stand, I take my tray to the counter and hurry out of the lunchroom, heading for the nearest girl's bathroom. I find an empty stall in the corner behind the baffle wall and lean back against the door. My throat aches big time but I refuse to start yodeling here.

Stalking the team? Twice I've encountered them, the second time totally by accident. And there was no one around to tell anyone about that! Jarrett? Would he really make fun of me like that?

Other girls are coming and going. In the stall next to me, now there are three pairs of feet and plumes of cigarette smoke. In a few minutes, they leave.

I hear snatches of conversation, fading in and out as girls come in, pee, fix makeup and hair, you know, the girly stuff, then leave. I don't recognize the voices.

"...her computer taken away, can't have it in her room anymore."

"...because she was sending naked pictures of herself. You saw that, right?"

"...said so and she would know. She heard it..."

"...Well believe it. Close-ups even..."

"...As if she could get him away from Laurie Ann..."

You don't have to be on the Principal's List to figure out it's me they're talking about. And there's only one person who knows I don't have a computer in my room.

The bathroom quiets and the class bell rings. It's safe to come out so I go to a sink and scour my makeup off. Then I stick out my tongue at the freckled face in the mirror, and tell her, "You're still Lisa! Did you really think a little makeup would change anything?"

# 2

I CAN'T GO TO CLASS. I can't face anyone. I just know I have to get away. I exit the bathroom and leave the school at a run, without going up to my locker. My books, backpack, even my jacket are left behind.

I jog almost the whole way home. Even with the exercise, I'm soon sorry I hadn't gone up for my jacket and I'm really wishing the lacy shirt was warmer. Once home, I pull it off, throw it over the back of my desk chair to dry, and pull on a big shapeless sweatshirt before grabbing my barn coat and going out to Wembly's stall.

I haven't stripped it yet. Haven't wanted to. That would make it too real. Too final. But I can't feel his presence any more. There's just emptiness. With the fork and the wheelbarrow, I get to work hauling every piece of manure, every sign of sawdust, every scrap of leftover hay, to the manure pile. Then I take a rubber feed bucket to Wembly's grave, up-end it and sit on it, ignoring the drizzle and the darkening sky, welcoming the cold.

After a bit, lights go on in the house, and although I hear Mom calling, I can't make myself get up. Then, there's Mom with a raincoat over her head, coming out of the house and heading toward the barn, still calling.

I get up, grab the bucket and go back inside the barn through Wembly's old stall just as Mom comes in the other door.

"Lisa, what on earth are you doing? You're soaking wet. Didn't you hear me calling? I thought you were going to start the potatoes."

"Sorry. Forgot."

"Well, thanks a lot. I got dinner myself. And it's ready. So let's go."

Once at the table, I pick at potatoes and some salad before scraping my plate into Big Mutt's dish and going to my room.

No backpack = no homework. I finish reading *The Hunger Games*.

When the house is quiet, I get Mom's big scissors from the sewing room, go into the bathroom and put the wastebasket up on the counter. I pull my hair back into a pony tail, cut it off, and drop it in the wastebasket. When I use the hand mirror to examine the results, I have to admit it didn't work out as well as I'd hoped. I scissor away until it's short all around, with the top just a bit longer. There! Good! I clean up the hair that missed the wastebasket, and shampoo as I shower.

"WHAT HAVE YOU DONE to your hair?" Mom shrieks when I come down for breakfast the next morning. Dad and Jemmy, sitting at the island counter, look up from their bowls and stare.

"Just got tired of it," I say. I shrug and give everyone a smile. "No big deal."

"No big deal? It looks like it's been rat chewed! I'm going to phone and see if I can get you in for a hair appointment *today*."

"No, it's okay Mom." I'm actually pretty pleased with my new look. All I'd done that morning was wet it, comb some gel through, and tousle. The little bit of natural curl made the style quite nice, in my opinion.

"Well," Dad says, "I agree it doesn't need to be any shorter, but it does need some work. You can't go around looking like something the cat dragged in."

"I like it!" Jemmy chimes in, cutting off any points Dad might've wanted to make regarding a young lady and finesse.

"You look like a boy!"

"Chill, Dad! Gotta run!" I grab a jacket and bolt out the door heading for the bus stop before there can be any more discussion about going to the hair dresser, or why I would cut it myself in the first place. Or my obvious lack of finesse.

When the bus stops in front of the school, I plod along with the rest of the students, but instead of going up to my locker, I turn left and go to the office. I've forged a note to cover my absence yesterday afternoon and I drop it off in the appropriate basket on the counter.

The fake signature won't fool anyone, but it's worked in the past, so I'm not worried. The trick of course is to never turn in a note actually signed by your mother. Since the beginning of the year, all notes have been mine. Not that there have been many. I'm also counting on no one comparing the excuse notes to signatures on report cards, and the secretaries all being too busy to phone my parents to confirm. Being an A-average student has its perks, the main one being that the secretaries don't pay much attention to the notes. I think they just glance at them and do whatever they need to do in the computer, then toss them. I'm guessing about that, of course. If they keep them somewhere, like for instance in a Lisa Rogney's Life in High School file, then someday someone may compare them to report cards, or notice they look different than notes from last year when I was so naïve I turned in actual notes from Mom. I'll be in trouble then! I'm not worried about it, though, because what could they do? Unless of course I have my driver's license by then and my parents won't let me use one of their cars for a while. That would suck! But it's months away so I don't dwell on it.

You might be surprised to know that despite yesterday's events, I'm still committed to becoming more like the "in crowd". After all, no one would really believe those boobs were mine. So the truth will come out pretty quickly.

This morning, obviously my little girl French braid is gone. I'm wearing leggings and a nice tunic top. No cowboy boots! I start up the stairs. Laurie Ann and Zelda pass me on their way down. Both hiss "Fuckin' skank!" as they go by. I just squeeze over to the right, well out of hip-check range, but otherwise ignore them.

Like yesterday in the lunchroom, there's twittering and giggling as I pass. I guess it'll take a little longer for everyone to get over the boob photo. I go through the fire doors from the stairwell and into the hall. There's a noisy crowd around my locker. When I get near, the kids all scatter, and I see what the excitement is about. I'm frozen and just stand there looking at my locker door. Someone has used lipstick to write "i suck" on it, and there's a long, squiggly arrow pointing to a penis.

For a heartbeat, I'm paralyzed and just stare at it. Then I root a Kleenex out of my backpack and wipe at it. The lipstick smears and the Kleenex is covered in it before I make much progress.

I'm aware the girl with the locker next to mine, Angie Clark, the girl I mentioned I was going to ask to eat lunch with me, has come up beside me and is looking at me. I turn her way a bit and she says, "I don't know who did it. I just got here."

"I know." I feel my shoulders slump. I try to smile at her and ask: "Have you got any Kleenexes?"

Angie rifles through a bin in her locker, then her purse, and comes up with a few more tissues. Like the first, these just smear everything.

"Must have used up an entire tube," I say. I'm guessing; I don't know how much painting you can do with a tube of lipstick. I imagine it depends on whether it was a new, full tube or not. Anyway, the Kleenex isn't going to take care of it. It's only a minute to class bell, so I decide that at lunch I'll go to the office and ask them to send the custodian.

"You got most of, er, *it*, anyway," Angie says, "and I guess this is not the best time to say it, but I like your hair."

Not the best time? I'm really glad to hear her say that. "Thanks, Angie."

We both grab our books and head into home room.

# 4

I'D LIKE TO SAY I put the graffiti out of my mind because it's just so juvenile, but my thoughts keep returning to it. I should've gone straight to the office and reported it. I'll go as soon as the lunch bell goes.

I should probably tell them about yesterday's cafeteria incident, the boob photo, too, but of course I won't, for two reasons: one, I'd sound like a whiney baby; and two, nobody likes a rat.

I realize I don't have to do anything. The lipstick isn't gone but it's smeared to nothing. The custodian will clean it off tonight. It's a mean thing to do to someone, though. Why me? I tell myself I don't care. I don't care. I don't care!

"Earth calling Lisa!" I realize the teacher is calling me. Apparently, this is not the first time she called.

"I—er, sorry! I missed the question." I feel heat creeping up my neck and know my face is turning red. Thankfully only a few students turn to look at me.

Ms. Fisher says, "Okay, someone tell Space Cadet Rogney what the question was."

Short Grain always wants to answer every question, so Ms. Fisher usually tries someone else first. But as usual, his is the only hand up. She acknowledges him.

"When a paired allele for a certain trait is heterozygous, what are the three possible, er, expressions?" he says. His voice is squeaky and girlish. As usual, the F-average boys in the back snicker, and I notice the back of Short Grain's neck and his prominent ears turning pink.

Ms. Fisher says, "Lisa?"

"I don't know."

"Did you read the assigned chapters?"

"No. Sorry."

Ms. Fisher frowns at me for a heartbeat, then turns to the class: "Who knows? Anyone?"

Again, it's Short Grain. "Complete dominance, co-dominance, and incomplete dominance."

He would know. Nerd. But at least he didn't let the snickering shut him up.

You're probably wondering why I call him Short Grain. He's in my biology class so obviously I know his real name. In fact, I didn't come up with Short Grain until I found out his last name was Rice, and then it was just obvious. He's a weedy little guy with thick glasses that make his eyes appear watery and over-sized, heavy black rims enormous on his pinched-looking white face, taped together at the bridge. You can't make this stuff up! He's always in that same long-sleeved, grubby white dress shirt, his knobby little hands dangling from too-big cuffs, and he's always alone. He's even more of an outsider than I am. At least I'm too big to be stuffed in a locker.

I wonder why no one stopped them.

I wonder why I didn't.

The bell rings for lunch break and the race is on. Ms. Fisher shouts out the homework assignment, and then she adds: "Don't forget—quiz Monday!"

All at once, thirty kids all head for the door. There's squawking and laughing and desk legs scraping the floor; everyone's in a panic to get out. You'd think they're afraid they'll be locked in and made to listen to bagpipe music if they're too slow. Short Grain has to be careful because being so small, he could be trampled in the stampede.

Don't get me wrong, I don't want to be left behind either, so I'm right in there with the other kids. I just get up beside Ms. Fisher's desk when she says, "Lisa! A word?"

Am I seriously in trouble for not reading the assigned chapter the night before? Does she remember I missed yesterday's class? Could she possibly have checked with the office, and figured out my excuse note is a fake?

But once the classroom has emptied and I'm standing in front of her desk, I see she has a soft look around her eyes. She asks, "Something going on, Lisa? It's not like you to be absent so much and miss assignments. I thought you liked biology class."

"I do! After Art, it's my favourite." Ms. Fisher, aside from being the prettiest teacher in the school, is also very nice and has as much finesse as a young lady can get, in my opinion. Not that she's young; she's totally old, maybe even thirty almost, but you know, compared to the other teachers. You probably think I'm a suck-up, but she's been my favourite teacher since Grade Nine. I don't want her to think badly of me and I wish I could come up with a convincing excuse, but I don't know how I can without admitting what's been going on. So, I just shake my head and say, "Sorry. I'll catch up."

Ms. Fisher looks as if she might say something more, but instead she nods and says, "Okay."

Dismissed, I escape the classroom and trot up to my locker. Thankfully, there are only a few kids scattered around. Everything's back to normal.

Except.

On my locker door, in lipstick a darker shade than before, it's all back. This time, "L.R. + J.M." inside a heart, is added.

Before I can gather my thoughts, I hear Jarrett shout, "Lisa!" I turn and see him striding toward me, scowling, his fists opening and closing. I back up a couple of steps until I come up against a locker.

He stops up close and snarls, "You fuckin' trying to ruin my life?"

He slams the heel of his hand on the locker very close to my head. The locker door responds with a loud, tinny bang. He leaves his hand there and stands rigid. "Laurie Ann was pissed enough before! Now she's fuckin' ballistic!"

"I didn't do it! It was just there—"

"Don't give me that!"

"Jarrett, I didn't do it! Why would I? Why would any sane person? Besides, I don't even own a lipstick!"

"A hundred people fuckin' saw you!" At least he hasn't had Caesar salad recently, and I'm glad about that, but he's talking so fast and so loud, and he's so close, he's spraying droplets of spit on my face.

"Eww! Boy germs!" I say, and try to move away.

Jarrett's frown deepens; he puts his other hand on the locker, penning me completely in. "You better

fuckin' hope she doesn't break up with me over this!"
he hisses. More spittle.

Then he's quiet but for his heavy breathing; in a
moment, he delivers another punch to the locker before
he straightens, looks around the hall at the dozen or so
kids watching, drops his arms, turns and strides away.

I slump back, close my eyes and rub my face. I
can feel my heart thumping. I actually hear my own
pulse. Stunned, I watch Jarrett's receding back and try
to block out the amused tittering of the staring kids.
Where is the Jarrett I've known half of my life? Dozens
of times over the years "boy germs" or "girl germs" was
a joke between us, and now it's not funny?

The day custodian, the cheerful female one, is
pushing the janitor's cart toward me. "Oh, yeah, here it
is. Someone made a mess of your locker, eh?" she says
with a chuckle as she takes a bottle of some lemony
chemical cleaner and sprays the locker front. "You
know who?"

I shake my head.

"Of course not. Nobody seen who done it.
Nobody knows nothing," she's grousing, but she smiles
at me and attacks the lipstick with paper towels.

I go to the stairwell and trot down to the landing
to wait out of sight while my locker is cleaned. I'm
shaking now, a result of adrenalin, I guess. I sit on the

window ledge, take a few deep breaths and wait for the adrenalin to subside. Jarrett! Does having your girlfriend mad at you really ruin your life? If that's what the "in crowd" is like, do I even want to try to be part of it?

I give my new short hairdo a vigorous, all-over, two-handed ruffling and take lots of gulping breaths. I don't want to start yodeling here, even though it's just hit me: there's no hope, I've lost my two best friends, three if you count Wembly, and except for Wembly, I don't know why.

I also don't know why everyone's so mean. Maybe it isn't nice giving people Temporary Names like Fido and Short Grain, but those are really like pet names, after all. Zelda and the other witch names not so much. But I never call them that to their faces except that one time I mentioned, and I'd never do anything like the boob photo or the penis locker!

I guess I just can't fit in. The best thing for me to do is to stay on the DL. Down Low. Invisible.

CR℘CR

# FOUR

## 1

FRIDAY, LUNCH TIME. The book sale is underway, but most of the activity is around the cookie table. Laurie Ann and Nicole are in the cookie-table crowd, so it's easy to stay out of their sight. I'm staying on the DL. I'm so DL I'm invisible. I've melted into the student masses.

I'm at the book tables, poking through the piles in hopes of finding something to replace *The Hunger Games Trilogy* I just finished reading. I strike gold! A first edition of *Cat's Eye*. Margaret Atwood is my all-time, most favourite author since *A Handmaid's Tale* was on the optional reading list last fall.

If I don't become an artist, maybe I could be a writer. Dad has made it clear he's not on board with me studying art in university because I need to take courses that will qualify me for a Real Job. Writing courses would be much better, right? With a BA in English under my belt, I would not only qualify for Real Jobs, but whenever there was a lull in the conversation, I'd be able to come out with witty quotes and authors' names complete with titles of their books.

I should admit here that Margaret Atwood isn't my only all-time, most favourite author. I have a few, just like I have lots of all-time, most favourite songs and two all time, most favourite sandwiches. But a Margaret Atwood book collection would be a great thing for an aspiring novelist to have. I already have *A Handmaid's Tale* so I'm off to a good start. I'll take it with me to whatever college I go to, to get the education I need for the Real Job I'll have to get to support myself until my writing career takes off.

I check the book for loose pages or other damage. It falls open at page a hundred and ninety-seven, the start of chapter thirty-seven, and I read the first couple of paragraphs. No dangling participles for Ms. Atwood! I never let my participles dangle either and the fact I know about these things bodes well for my future as a writer. If you think I mentioned "dangling participles" just because I like the way those words sound and go together, High Five to you!

Anyway. The book. The reason it fell open to this page is that it's coming away from its binding there. I decide I'm going to buy it anyway, when suddenly I'm bumped by the person on my right. Not like she just brushed up against me accidentally, although even that would be rude. It's Zelda.

This is enough book sale. I turn away and head for the cashier. I haven't gone more than half a dozen steps when I'm given a hard shove from behind and I'm propelled into the crowd. I stumble. Can't get my feet under me. The kids scatter like bowling pins and in the blink of an eye I'm on all fours on the floor. *Cat's Eye* is lying open, probably at page one ninety-seven, nearby. Pink Skechers pass in a blur of feet around me. I sit back on my haunches in time to see Nicole, with Laurie Ann and Zelda, pushing through the crowd, rushing away.

There's another girl sitting on the floor close to me. She looks surprised. Somehow when I fell, my face hit something. I'm guessing it was her. "Are you okay?" I ask. She answers with a tentative nod and although she seems stunned, with the help of her friend she manages to get to her feet.

I'm a bit light headed and need a minute before I can get up. Something drips from my nose. I wipe at it with the back of my hand and see it's blood. Then Ms. Fisher is crouching beside me. She hands me a Kleenex and asks, "What happened?"

"I fell. I think I hit her," I nod toward the other girl, who is now surrounded by friends, seemingly unfazed. With the Kleenex to my nose, I retrieve *Cat's Eye* and get to my feet.

"Yes," Ms. Fisher continues, "but why? Did you trip on something?"

"I—I don't know—it happened so fast." I draw a deep breath. The Kleenex is saturated, and blood is once again dripping, now staining my shirt. I feel light-headed again.

Ms. Fisher takes my elbow and helps me up. "You look pale," she says, and hands me another tissue. "People!" she shouts. "Anyone see what happened?"

She is answered by a chorus of murmurs. No one speaks up. She frowns, shakes her head and turns back to me. "Are you okay?"

"I think so, except for this nosebleed. Would you have more Kleenex?"

"Come with me." Ms. Fisher takes my arm and guides me toward the office.

"My book! I haven't paid for it."

Ms. Fisher takes it from me and holds it up for the cashier to see as we pass. Once through the office into the nurse's room, I sit as instructed, take a couple of fresh tissues from the dispenser and hold the wad against my nostrils.

Ms. Fisher gets a cloth from the cabinet, runs it under cold water, wrings, folds, and places it on my face across my nose. "I wish the nurse was here today," she says. "I think you need to be looked at. Can I call someone for you?"

"Thanks, but no one's home now anyway. I think the bleeding's stopping. I'll call Dad if I feel like I need to."

"I still want to know how it happened," Ms. Fisher says. "I don't think you just fell over your own two feet! If something's going on, Lisa, I hope you know you can tell me."

I move the cool cloth up so it also covers my eyes, take several deep mouth-breaths and consider telling Ms. Fisher everything. But it's embarrassing. And I don't want to be a tattletale. This is a problem I have to solve on my own.

"Can you at least tell me why you've missed so many classes?"

"I ... well," I take the cloth away from my face and wad up the soiled Kleenexes. "My horse, Wembly. He died a couple weeks ago." A sob catches in my throat. Despite my best efforts, I can feel my lower lip start to tremble. I grab it in my teeth before it really gets going.

Pulling her chair around so we're face to face, Ms. Fisher grasps my forearm. "I'm sorry. People may tell you it's just an animal but it's a big part of your life gone. It's only natural to grieve." She takes her hand away, gives my arm a rub, and straightens. "But I wonder if it isn't more than that, Lisa. You can tell me when you're ready. In the meantime, you can lie down, stay here until dismissal if you want. If the nosebleed gets worse again, sit up." She hands me the book. "I'll go pay for this. You can pay me back next week," she says, and leaves. I manage to remember to thank her before the door closes behind her.

I get on the cot and lie with the cool cloth on my face. I tried to stay on the Down Low, but I guess I can't make myself invisible. I tried. They found me.

# 2

FRIDAY IS AN EARLY dismissal day. At final bell, I get up, look out the window and see the school bus already at the curb. As I mentioned, the way to the nurse's room is through the office. One of the secretaries looks up when I emerge and wants to know what happened. I can't be rude and not answer, so I tell her what I told Ms. Fisher. Not the Wembly part, just how it happened fast and so on.

Then the librarian and a math teacher come in and I have to go through the same story again. It seems all the teachers heard about The Book Sale Incident. They must have their own Teacher Grapevine, because I don't think they really listen to the kid gossip. Or do they?

Anyway. They're all oohing and I'm sorry-ing, I hope you're okay-ing, I could call your mother or father-ing and so on. I thank them, assure them I'm fine, and finally escape before more teachers show up.

The bus waits for no one, so now I'm in a hurry to get to my locker. I try to trot up the stairs, and quickly realize the fall hurt more than my nose. Needles of pain shoot through my left knee and instead of trotting, I'm barely able to hobble. I grip the handrail. Stinging pain starts in my shoulder, too. I won't be jogging home today! Just climbing two flights of stairs is taxing.

But by the time I get my books in my backpack and hobble back down to the front entrance, the bus is half a block away. I drop my backpack on the step and put on my jacket. I pull the hood over my head, hoist my backpack, and start out on another long walk home. I only go as far as the end of the front lawn when I realize I'm really not up to an hour's walk.

I sit on the retaining wall that divides the lawn from the parking lot and text Dad. If you want a ride from Dad, Friday is a good day to ask for it, because he likes an excuse to leave early. From the sounds of it, his office is pretty well empty except for the secretaries by three every Friday. He texts back that he's on his way.

I've only been waiting a couple of minutes when two boys in basketball team jackets come out the side door. There are girls with them. Both couples are holding hands. As they walk out into the parking lot, I recognize them: Jarrett and Laurie Ann. Tyler and Nicole.

Jarrett and Laurie Ann is nothing worth mentioning, but Tyler and Nicole? That's new! Then I notice Nicole's pink shoes. The pieces fall into place. I realize how far my once-best friend is willing to go to be part of The Coven.

They pass within five meters of where I am, but if they notice me, they don't let on.

Have you ever seen a documentary about primitive cultures, like those deep in the jungles of New Guinea? I'm thinking of the ones that punish bad people, say like murderers or someone who disrespected the chief or did something else that is taboo, by telling them they're dead? Then everyone in the tribe goes on living, doing their hunting and gathering and passing by them hundreds of times, but no one ever acknowledges even seeing them. They sit outside the wall or the gate or the circle of huts, whatever they have, and die.

I know how they must feel.

# 3

I know, I kind of left that thought out there, and it's a bad thought for sure. If you think I'm going to go away and die, you can forget it. It was only a temporary low feeling, and you know when you feel low, there's nowhere to go but up!

I have to tell Mom and Dad about falling, for two reasons: one, Dad wants to know why I'm too sore to walk home (being as I've done it so many times); and two, my nose is swollen and my eyes are both turning black. I don't tell them I think Nicole pushed me down, though. They would report it to the principal, right after they went over to Nicole's house and made a big fuss about it with her parents, then her parents would be really mad at her and who knows what they might do! Likely they'd ground her, not let her borrow the car, take away her credit card if she got it, or all three. You can see why it would really piss Nicole off. There'd be no chance I could still be friends with her again after I ratted her out like that. I mean, ever.

Besides, I just can't believe Nicole did it, and I'm not a hundred percent sure it was her, either. It could have been Zelda. She's the one who shoved me at the book table, after all.

I'm sore all over and my knee hurts when I move it certain ways, but I don't make too much fuss about it. I'm excused from my usual Saturday household chores because I whined a little, but I have to be careful because if I make too big a fuss about it, they'll insist on taking me to have it X-rayed, and Mom and Dad have too many things to do on their days off to spend hours waiting in Emergency.

If you think maybe I don't want to waste my time at the hospital either, well, High Five to you, but at least there was a thought for my parents in there. It's not really all that sore, but if it's still hurting after a few days, like on a school day, I'll make a fuss about it then.

4

I STAY IN MY JAMMIES, prop myself up on my bed with a bag of frozen peas on my knee, and start reading *Cat's Eye*. A while ago, like maybe just before Christmas, I would've thought the scene where young Elaine Risley is lured to the ice in the gully by her friends then left helpless is too fake, even though as you know I have this big respect and admiration for Margaret Atwood. But what they did was evil, and they're just kids. Now I believe kids are capable of it.

There's a tap on my door. It opens and Mom sticks her head in.

"Lisa," she says, "Doctor Bennie's on the phone, and wants to talk to you."

"Me? What for?"

"Ask him yourself." She hands me the phone.

I take it and say, "Hello?"

"Hi Lisa. It's Doctor Bennie."

"Hi."

"You know, I wanted to tell you again how sorry I am about Wembly. He was a good boy."

"Thank you." I manage to choke the words out around the lump that suddenly materializes in my throat again.

"I know it's only been a few weeks, but, well, I have a favour to ask of you."

"A favour?"

"You can say no, and please do if I'm asking too much, but I wouldn't ask if we weren't desperate." He clears his throat. "I volunteer with the horse and donkey rescue. You know of it?"

"Umm. I guess I've heard of it. Haven't really thought about it though."

"Well, besides going to auctions and buying horses that are being bid on by meat buyers, they take animals that've been apprehended because of neglect or abuse."

"Oh? Well, that's good. Really good."

"Yeah. But the need is great, and right now, they're full. They have a donkey that needs a temporary home and someone to care for her until she's fit for adoption and a permanent home can be found for her. I said I knew of someone who might be willing to take her."

"Oh. You mean, us?"

"It's not meant to replace Wembly, you understand. It's just, well, this little donkey really needs someone to take care of her until she's better. She's not adoptable as she is now."

"Maybe. I mean I think so. I'll have to check with my parents."

"I've already talked to your mother and she's given her blessing. Provided you will make the commitment."

"Well, then," I look at Mom, who's hovering nearby. "We have hay ... and an empty stall ... Yes!"

"Keep in mind she's injured, and she'll need the wound dressings changed, at first daily. It's not pretty. I'll show you what to do and provide all the supplies, but you'll need a strong stomach!"

"I think I'll be okay with it."

"I'm sure you will. I remember you helping me with Wembly a couple of times. When can we bring her? Is this afternoon too soon?"

"No. I'll have the stall ready."

"Okay great! Look for us in about an hour. And prepare yourself for a very pathetic little donkey." He hangs up.

"They're bringing her in an hour!" I tell Mom. "I have to get dressed, check the paddock to make sure it's okay, and get some bedding in the stall! Thank you thank you thank you!"

I get up off the bed, give Mom and quick hug and hand the phone back to her. She leaves.

I paw through the clothes on the floor of my closet, throw on grubby jeans and a T-shirt, then head downstairs and out the door, grabbing my barn coat on the way.

I definitely don't want to be re-assigned those household chores I mentioned, so I'm careful to limp now and then until I'm out of view.

# 5

DOCTOR BENNIE'S TRICKED out vet truck rolls into our yard half an hour late, followed by a truck and trailer driven by someone I haven't seen before. Doctor Bennie, slightly rotund in his overalls, says, "Sorry we're late. We had a little trouble getting her to load." Then he introduces the driver, Rick somebody. I don't catch his last name. How could I? He is breathtaking. Tall. Lean. Gray green eyes that sparkle with his big grin. No overalls here, just snug jeans, a T-shirt, and hip-length jacket with "Wrangler" embroidered in big writing down the sleeve. Wide shoulders. Narrow hips. I get a funny feeling deep inside and just stare, speechless. I cringe. He must think I'm a drooling idiot. Well, maybe not drooling, but definitely an idiot.

I didn't catch his last name, as I mentioned, but I immediately think of Shawn Seville. You know, the star of South Side High? I don't like the show much but if you think I watch it once in a while just to see Shawn, High Five to you. So he'll be Rick Seville to me and I might watch South Side High more often now and picture him in there doing all the stuff Shawn does, like smooching Adele. I sometimes imagine I'm Adele and Shawn is smooching me. Although she's only into the smooching once in a while and I would always be totally into it. I don't know how she can be so mean to Shawn.

Anyway. When I tune back in, Doctor Bennie is explaining that Rick is working part time at the clinic to help pay for vet school. Rick opens the man door at the front of the trailer, steps inside, and I can hear him talking in a soft voice to the donkey. I'm guessing he's untying her, because Doctor Bennie goes to the big back doors and calls out, "Ready?"

Rick says he is, so Doctor Bennie opens the doors. Rick has the donkey's lead rope and turns her around so she can come out by walking forward rather than backing out.

She is so small! And she has a bandage that nearly covers her front leg. She's nervous about coming out of the trailer.

"I don't think she trusts that leg to hold her," Doctor Bennie says.

Rick Seville and Doctor Bennie support her and between them, manage to coax her out.

Rick Seville hands the lead rope to me. "Lead the way, Lisa!" he says, and give me a big, Crest White Strips ad grin. Suddenly I'm very warm. I take the lead rope without even realizing what I'm doing. I can't tear my eyes off of Rick. He's staring at me, too. Totally checking me out!

I give myself a mental kick and tell myself to act like I'm used to boys gawking at me like that. I turn to scratch the donkey's withers. I tell her: "It's okay, little one. You're safe now," and lead her into Wembly's old stall.

We all watch as the little donkey checks out her new surroundings. When she seems content, I clip the lead on her halter again, and bring her out into the alleyway so Doctor Bennie can tend her wound. He carefully cuts away the dressing, exposing a festering, swollen mass of raw meat.

When Doctor Bennie said I'd need a strong stomach, he wasn't kidding. Mom looks a bit green and decides it's a good time to go back to the house. I'm feeling queasy myself but I'm not going to let on. I go to the far side of the donkey, which isn't the greatest from a learning what to do viewpoint as I can't see what's going on from there, but it's enough that I get my lunch back down in my stomach where it belongs before Doctor Bennie says I should come around to his side so he can show me what to do.

I'm trying to absorb all that Doctor Bennie is telling me, but it's really not easy keeping focused when Rick Seville is so close. He's standing right beside me, practically close enough to touch! Why had I just thrown on my ratty old barn jeans? I could just as easily have worn the skinny jeans with the stylish little rips and fancy butt pockets! Maybe the T-shirt with the lacy cut-outs, too, cleavage or no cleavage.

Doctor Bennie comments on how good the little donkey is, standing so nice and still. "It must be painful, even with the pain meds she's on, no matter how carefully it's done." Then, as he's doling out gauze and vet wrap, this ointment and that, Doctor Bennie says, "By the way, Lisa, looks like you've had a painful experience lately."

I was so wrapped up in Rick Seville, the donkey, what Doctor Bennie was telling me, but mostly Rick Seville, I'd forgotten about my face. I get a sinking feeling. No wonder he was staring at me!

I wish the ground would open up and swallow me. Now my face must be black, blue AND red. They're both looking at me, expecting an explanation. "You should see the other guy!" I tell them. Then, seeing as neither of them is going to let me off the hook, I add: "I fell."

"Oh? How?" Rick asks.

"Just ... oh you know, I wasn't watching where I was going." So now Rick Seville thinks I'm a drooling idiot *and* a klutz.

"Okay," Doctor Bennie says, "As long as it wasn't horse related!"

"Definitely not horse related." I hear myself sigh.

When he's finished, Doctor Bennie promises to stop by every week, and tells me to call his cell if I have any problems or questions. Then he says, "See you next week", and leaves. I wonder if Rick Seville will stop by, too. He doesn't say he will, but he doesn't say he won't, either. He gives me a wink before getting in his truck.

I remember that wink far too many times over the following days, and every time I do, I get that same warm stirring deep, you know, down there.

# FIVE

## 1

ANGIE CLARK AND I have no classes together, but since our lockers are side by side, we've known each other since the beginning of the year. I gave her a Temporary Name, but it was very temporary because she's nice and friendly and introduced herself right away.

If you're wondering what I Temporary Named her, it was Latoya, because she totally looks how Latoya Martinez would if she didn't wear so much make-up and of course didn't have a pierced nose, eyebrows, lips and so on. Also of course if Latoya had dark skin and curly black hair. In other words, she's gorgeous.

I might not have introduced myself to her and we might have just gone on nodding to each other all year, because I thought someone so beautiful would be stuck-up and would have lots of friends of the popular variety, so she wouldn't have a minute for someone like me who as I've mentioned, totally lacks finesse, even though back then I did have a couple of friends.

Angie is someone your parents would be glad to have you hang with and Dad would see she already has a lot of finesse, maybe because she went to private school until her family moved here last fall.

You might be thinking she was only friendly to me because she didn't know anyone else, but Angie's not like that. She made other friends right away, too, but she still does stuff with me, like walking over to the Pita Pit for lunch, or sometimes after school we walk home together, at least until I have to turn to go onto the Parkway path. She also asks me to come along when she's doing stuff with her other friends.

Since the Lipstick Penis Incident, she's been spending less time with her other friends and more time with me, including our lunch hours. Today, the lunchroom is crowded and noisy. We find empty seats in the far corner. A few seats away, as far into the corner as is possible, sits Short Grain. As usual, he's alone. As usual, he's reading.

"How's the little donkey doing?" Angie asks.

"Better. Her coat doesn't look as rough as it did, and the dressings aren't all soaked with blood and pus when I take them off. The wound looks pink. Doctor

Bennie calls it 'pinking up'. And it seems to be closing."

Just two more visits from Doctor Bennie, and I've totally learned what to do. He says he won't need to come so often any more. This sounds like it's a really good thing, because it must mean the wound is coming along and he must think I'm doing a good job, but I'll miss Doctor Bennie's visits just the same.

If you think it's really Rick Seville's visits I'll miss, you can forget it, because he hasn't been back. Not even once.

"It's only been a couple weeks, but Doctor Bennie says she had a body score of two out of ten when they found her, and with that wound, was considered for euthanasia. So she's coming along nicely and is a very a lucky girl. I thought I knew what to expect, but it was worse. Way worse." I dig into my all-time most favourite sandwich, peanut butter and dill pickle on multigrain.

I see Short Grain has looked up from his book and is listening to what we're talking about. Maybe it's a little graphic, but it's not like I came out with something like the mouse in the stew limerick that bothered a certain person, and he doesn't have to listen in, after all.

"Hi," I say, "not a great lunch-time conversation. Sorry."

He nods, starts turning red, and mumbles something like, "It's okay. I'm interested."

Of course he's interested, biology nerd that he is. But everyone knows even if you're sitting right next to someone in the lunch room, which he isn't, given the vacant seats between him and me, you don't gawk and listen in on their conversation.

Still, the expression on his face reminds me of Big Mutt when he was so little we still called him Bodinga and he got caught piddling on the floor, so I can't be mad. I don't know what else to do, so I go with: "I'm in your biology class. This is Angie, and I'm Lisa."

"Ahem … Jimmy …" he says, almost in a whisper. Then he clears his throat again and says in a louder voice that starts off kind of deep but switches to squeaky at the end: "Jimmy." He's blushing like crazy now.

I jabber on. "We were just talking about a donkey that's at my place because they didn't have room for her at the rescue. She was a bone rack when she came. Abandoned when her owners were evicted. You wouldn't believe how heartless people can be." Then I remember the locker-stuffing incident and realize he probably would. I don't want him to think about that; he's already deep red and would only have purple to go to from here, so to keep his mind off it I rush on: "I've been taking care of her. She has a terrible gash on her leg."

Angie says, "Could I come and see her? I could help. Maybe Saturday?"

"Sure, that'd be great!" I agree. "Hope you have rubber boots! The yard's a quagmire in this rain."

Jimmy's staring, his eyes twice their actual size behind his thick lenses. It's not really rude now, because we did include him in the conversation. Not knowing what else to do, I ask him, "You wanna come too? The shit needs to be picked out of her paddock on Saturdays. Plenty of jobs to go around!"

This would be enough to make a sane person come up with tons of other things they have to do, like maybe they always vacuum the lint out of their pockets on Saturdays, but to my surprise, he nods vigorously. We agree on a time, and I give directions.

As I trot out to the school bus after school, I realize I'm humming. I have ignored Laurie Ann, Jarrett, The Coven, Jarrett, the basketball team—the whole damn works—for weeks! Even when they tittered and giggled about my face. I didn't even care when Valentine's Day came and went, and my only cards were from Angie and Jemmy. Or that I had no date for the dance. Or even a girlfriend to go solo with because Angie had a date. I didn't want to go anyway. Angie said I didn't miss anything.

# 2

SATURDAY AT THE AGREED TIME, Angie drives into the yard. She's a little older than I am, obviously, and got her driver's license as soon as she turned sixteen. Her mother lets her use the car so much it's as good as hers. If you think her mother doesn't care because her car's an old klunker anyway, you can forget it. It's real nice, with a back-up camera, heated leather seats, stereo speakers everywhere and so on. The only hitch is, Angie has to put gas in (with a credit card her mother gave her) and keep it clean. Which is totally not a big deal and worth it for sure.

If it sounds like I'm jealous, I am. If you're wondering why I can't borrow my mother's car, it's because I don't have my license yet. My birthday was a while ago and most other kids would have their license by the time they're my age. I have my learner's permit, but I've been too busy to do much practice driving. The times Mom can take me driving always seem to be when I have a scheduling conflict; school stuff mostly but sometimes horse stuff, and if you think I'll go driving with Dad, you can forget it. There's only so much swearing I can stand. I tell myself I'll hold off going for the road test until Mom gets a new car, one with a back-up camera, you know, for the parking part of the test.

She says she's probably going to get a new car soon. Probably before I turn a hundred.

"I wonder about Jimmy. How will he get here?" Angie asks almost as soon as she gets out of the car. She's always thinking of other people. Did I mention she's a very nice person?

"I didn't think to ask."

We see a small figure in dark clothing trudging along the road, but the city bus stop is in the opposite direction, so it isn't until he turns into the driveway, we realize it's Jimmy. Has he walked all the way? He's wearing a coat that must not be waterproof as it looks soaked through, and goofy rubber boots that are sort of floppy around the top and have metal clips up the front. I think maybe those clips close to stop the flopping.

The word *galoshes* pops into my mind even though I've never actually seen galoshes before. Galoshes is one of those words that's fun to say, and I love words like that, although words like galoshes hardly ever come up in conversation, so if you want to say galoshes, you have to make up a little poem about galoshes, such as:

When you're watering your squashes,
You should always wear galoshes.

My all time, most favourite word is Zimbabwe. It's a proper noun, but a proper noun's still a word so you can't disqualify it for that reason, and you have to admit Zimbabwe is super fun to say. The downside is, there is even less opportunity to say Zimbabwe than galoshes. Instead of a rhyming couplet for Zimbabwe, I've come up with a limerick:

A handsome young man from Zimbabwe
Sends texts as he cruises on Broadway.
When he raises his head
He sees the light's red
And pays for his error the hard way.

I imagine you have your own all-time, most favourite words. If so, you might want to make rhymes too, so whenever there's an awkward lull in the conversation you can come out with one. I find it puts people at ease.

Anyway. Jimmy's got those galoshes, and there's no hood on his coat and he doesn't have a hat, so his hair and glasses are rain wet and I wonder how he can even see where he's going. He must be cold and uncomfortable, but you wouldn't know it to look at him. He's grinning from ear to ear.

Together we walk up to the barn. Jenny peers through the boards on her stall when she hears us and gives a funny little grunting nicker.

"Jenny isn't her real name," I explain as I hook a lead rope onto her halter and bring her out to the crossties in the alleyway. "It's just temporary. We don't know her name. But she is a jenny, so ..."

"A Jenny?" Angie says.

"That's what a female donkey is called." This from Jimmy. "The males are jacks." That's Short Grain for you; he knows stuff. I've seen him in action in Biology class so I know about his mansplaining and don't hold it against him.

He starts in scratching Jenny's withers, which are just about at his eye level, and talking to her in what is most likely a very donkey-soothing voice. At least Jenny seems to be listening; she has one long ear tipped in his direction. "Who's a pretty girl, eh? Who's the prettiest?"

"Pretty?" Angie giggles, "she looks kind of ... well, goofy."

"She's not stupid, if that's what you're thinking," I say. It came out a little more sharply than I intended, so I give her a big grin and go cross-eyed to make sure she knows I'm not offended.

"Donkeys only look stupid," Jimmy says. "They're actually very smart. Hey, pretty girl?" He's moved his scratching hand to her domed forehead. If he wants to make friends with Jenny, or me for that matter, he's made a good start. I hand him a brush. He shucks his coat over the stall divider and asks for a hoof pick, and Angie and I watch as he picks up one foot after the other, cleaning them out.

"How come you know how to do that?" Angie asks.

"Before we moved here, our neighbours had animals," he explains. Then he points to the dressing on Jenny's leg. "What happened?"

"Nobody knows. Cut it on something. Doctor Bennie said she was rescued from a junkyard. Could've been anything." I put on surgical gloves and go to work, taking yesterday's dressing off. Next, I clean the wound, apply ointment, and wrap it back up again. When I'm done, I unclip the ties from Jenny's halter and pass the lead rope to Jimmy. "Could you please put her back in her stall while I deal with this mess?" I ask him. He looks like he won first prize, and all I did was let him lead Jenny. Some people are easily pleased. It's a nice quality.

I scoop up the soiled dressings and take them to the burn barrel outside. The surgical gloves come off

97

and go into the barrel too. When I come back in, we watch Jenny work away pulling hay out of the hay net for a few minutes.

"She sure is skinny!" Jimmy says.

"You should've seen her when she first came. She was so emaciated she could hardly get up on her own. Now Doctor Bennie says she'll soon be well enough to be adopted."

"You'll be glad about that, won't you?" Angie asks. "It seems like a lot of work."

"Hmm. I dunno. I think I'll miss her. She's really sweet. You should hear all the different sounds she makes! Almost like she's talking. Like this." I demonstrate by making donkey sounds. The nickering/snuffling I've got pretty well down pat, but if you've ever tried the "eee-haw" they make that sounds like someone using a hacksaw on a metal pipe, you know it's impossible, like imitating elephant trumpeting.

Angie and Jimmy both look like they don't know whether to laugh or run for the road. After a second, Angie attempts the eee-haw, then we're all doing it, and no one thinks about running for the road again. Except maybe Jenny.

Anyway. I go into the stall with Jenny, unhook the hay net and take it outside so she'll follow me and be out of the way. I give Angie the job of filling another hay net and get Jimmy sweeping the alleyway while I pick poo. When the wheelbarrow's full, Jimmy grabs the handles and humps it to the manure pile to dump, then loads it with clean sawdust and brings it back to tip in the stall.

With all the help, chores are done in record time. I hang the hay net Angie filled inside the stall, and say, "Okay! That's it! We're done already. Thanks for the help, guys! Let's go in the house and get warmed up. Mom baked cookies this morning."

I've mentioned Jimmy is small. He has a big appetite, though, and easily polishes off three mugs of hot chocolate and half a dozen cookies, if anyone's counting. He says, "Thanks, Mrs. Rogney! This is the best cocoa and these are the best cookies I've ever had."

Mom puts more cookies in a Ziplock bag and insists he take them home. You can read between the lines here: she gave them to Jimmy. Jimmy took them. No insisting required. What growing boy would argue? I wouldn't argue, and I'm done growing. I hope.

"Hey, Jimmy," Angie says as they're leaving, "You wanna lift home?"

# 3

ON MONDAY, ANGIE is waiting for me at our lockers. She doesn't say good morning or how are you today or any of the customary greetings. I expect more from a young lady who went to private school. She launches right in with: "Would you believe he lives all the way down in Black Diamond Park? I don't want to sound like a snob, but it sure is a crappy little shit hole of a house. Totally the opposite direction from here. And he didn't take the bus. He must've been walking for hours to get to your place."

"Why didn't he take the bus?"

"He said something about the bus schedule not working out, but I think he wanted to save the money."

I get a sinking feeling. "OMG."

"Well," Angie says, "next time, I'm gonna pick him up."

"Next time?"

"Yeah, of course, next time."

"You want to come again? Even with all the shit and muck?"

"Well, I know I wasn't much help, but I like Jenny, and I had fun! I haven't laughed so much in ages! You are the weirdest person I've ever known!"

You have to admit it's weird to tell someone they're weird and I must be giving her a hurt feelings look because she hurries on: "No, no! I mean weird in a good way! And Jimmy likes the idea of coming every Saturday. He said he had fun, too, but I think he's also hoping for more cookies. All the way to his house he was holding that baggie like it was treasure. I'm thinking those might be the only home-made cookies he's ever had. You should see where he lives! I'm not kidding, a 'Park' it is not. I would *not* want to go there after dark!"

As we're both pulling our books for the morning classes out of our lockers, I notice a doodle on the back of my math notebook. I was fooling around with it last week while I was waiting for the History teacher to quit droning on and on. There's an empty word balloon above an exaggerated long face with equally long nose, and ears nearly the same length as his head. I didn't start off drawing Tyler, it just ended up looking like him. So I gave him a basketball in each of his extra long, skinny hands. "Hey, check this out!" I show her. "I couldn't come up with anything brilliant for him to be saying. Ideas?"

Between the two of us, we come up with: *"I have rubber balls"*.

ରଃୠୠରଃ

# SIX

1

I'M QUITE LOOKING forward to school this morning. Well, not so much school although I do mostly like it, it's just the in-between stuff, you know, like what The Coven might come up with, I don't like.

I want to see Jimmy, because I have news. Doctor Bennie called last night to say a "furever" home had been found for Jenny. The new owners will take over her care and she can be moved to her new home on the weekend. Angie already knows about this because I texted her last night, but Jimmy doesn't have a phone. I can't wait to see the look on his face when I tell him!

I see Angie at our lockers first, of course. "It's so great!" she says, and we High Five. "That is such good news! Her own people to love her forever!"

"Doctor Bennie thought it would take much longer. I guess she's going to be a companion for an old horse. Let's go tell Jimmy!"

"Can't. Got homework to finish up before my first class."

"Okay. See you later."

There's still about fifteen minutes to bell, but Jimmy's usually early so I trot off. His locker is in the back wing and on the lower level, about as far from mine as you can get.

The basement hall is deserted. I put it down to the fact it's still early. But there are loud male voices just around the corner, in the short hall leading to the furnace room where Jimmy's locker is.

When I get to the corner, Tyler Robinson blocks my path. A little further past him, I see a scuffle in progress, with Jimmy in the middle of it.

"Stop it!" I yell. I try to go around Tyler, but he grabs my arm. Those long skinny hands I mentioned before are surprisingly strong. Maybe from holding onto basketballs so much. His fingers dig in, and I'm pretty sure I'm going to have bruises tomorrow.

"This is nothing for you to worry about," he says. "Stay the fuck out of it."

"They're hurting him!"

"None of your fuckin' business. Tell you what, though. We can have a little fun while we're waiting." He bodies me back against the wall and dives in like he's going to kiss me.

"Stop it!" I squirm out from under him and push him away, but I can't get his meat hooks off my arms.

"No? At least gimme a look at those tits. How're you hidin' them, anyway?"

The two other boys leave Jimmy and come toward us, heading for the main hall.

Tyler brings his face close to mine, narrows his eyes, and hisses, "You didn't see *nuthin'*." He finally drops my arm, turns and scurries off with the others.

I run to Jimmy, who is sitting on the floor, his backpack and its contents scattered around him. He gets to his feet, and I can see he's struggling not to cry. I pick up his glasses, which are now in three pieces, and hand them to him. Jimmy doesn't seem surprised they're broken; he roots a tube of Super Glue out of his backpack, peels the old tape off the bridge, and begins repairs, sniffling. I dig a Kleenex out of my purse and hand it to him. He honks into it and carries on fixing his glasses.

"Jimmy, why'd they jump you? What for?"

He's quiet, and although he's turned three-quarters away from me, I can see his shoulders moving as if he's trying not to yodel.

"Come on, Jimmy! They assaulted you! We need to report this!"

"No!" Now he turns his tear-streaked face to me. "That would just make it worse."

It dawns on me I'm in the same situation as Jimmy, and I don't want to tell anyone, either.

I let out a big sigh. "Okay, I get it. Why did they do it?"

"They ... they steal my homework."

"This happens every day?"

"No. Usually it's just my Chem homework, so, a couple times a week. And if I have a lunch, they take that." He takes a deep breath and wipes his sleeve across his face. "I try to be early enough to be outta here before they come."

Not satisfied the glue will hold, he digs a roll of adhesive tape and some small scissors out of his backpack, cuts a piece off, and wraps it carefully around the bridge. "They always dump my backpack because they never believe I don't have any money. Seems to piss them off."

Then puts his glasses on. With the addition of the new white tape, he looks like more of a caricature than ever. He gives me a puzzled look, as if he just realized it's unusual for me to be in this part of the school. "Why're you here?"

"Oh ... I came to tell you Jenny's been adopted. She's going to her new home this week-end." I give him a big smile and raise my hand, expecting a High Five.

But Jimmy turns away. "Oh," he says, his voice barely more than a whisper. "So you won't need me to help anymore."

I obviously haven't thought this through. I had no idea this was important to him. "Well, I hope you'll come and help strip her stall and everything. That is, if you want to. And if they didn't hurt you?"

He shakes his head. "I'm okay."

"Also, you might want to be there when they come to get her, you know, to say good-bye. I was thinking we might have a sort of send-off party."

"That would be great!" he says, pulling himself up straighter.

"Super! I'll get back to you with a time, when I know it." I turn, then look back and say, "See you at lunch!"

If you think I had a send-off party planned and just didn't mention it until now, you can forget it. I only got the idea when I saw how Jimmy's face fell. He was more upset about Jenny leaving and not being needed at my place than by what those bullies did.

It isn't until minutes later I rehash in my mind what Tyler did to me. If you think it was the first time a boy has tried to kiss me, you can forget that too, because Jarrett and I practiced kissing quite a lot. We started when we were about twelve and might be still at it if his family hadn't moved away. But that's different because I was as interested as he was. We probably had enough practice by the time he moved anyway because I was a pretty good kisser by then. I haven't had much practice since, but I suppose Jarrett is even better now because no doubt he's been at it with Laurie Ann. I'm not sure, but I have a feeling she might be a really good kisser, you know, *experienced*, because we've been in the same school since Grade Nine, and she's had a few boyfriends that I know of, while she is Jarrett's first girlfriend. She may have taught him a thing or two. So by now I'm falling way behind.

You probably figured out from other times I've mentioned Tyler I don't want him to kiss me, whether I need more practice or not. Did I do something to give him the idea I do? I mean, want him to kiss me, not need more practice. Maybe because of the Lipstick Penis incident? There's that Naked Boobs photo, although no one with a brain could think I'm hiding *those* somehow! I barely need a bra.

But since we're talking about brains, you have to keep in mind it's Tyler Robinson. He's one of the guys that always sits at the back of the class. You remember, one of the morons that tittered when Short Grain answered Ms. Fisher's question.

He pressed up against me when he was offering me the drugs, too, remember, and that was before Lipstick Penis and Naked Boobs. So maybe it's just Tyler.

Still, isn't he Nicole's boyfriend now? I wouldn't be happy if I had a boyfriend and he wanted to kiss and see the boobs of some other girl. I think maybe I should tell Nicole about it, but decide against it. She wouldn't believe me anyway and it would just make her hate me even more.

# 2

AT NOON, ANGIE and I find Jimmy in the lunchroom at his usual far corner seat and join him. He has no lunch, not surprising given the shakedown I witnessed. We each give him half a sandwich. I share my oatmeal raisin cookies; Angie splits her orange and says she doesn't want her granola dip. Jimmy says he's not hungry, but we don't believe him. Not hungry? Most days he's already eaten his lunch before we even get to the lunch room, and we've seen him in action on cookies at my place a few times after stall cleaning, so we know how much food he can maw down. We're not surprised when he makes short work of everything we push his way.

I'd already told Angie about the Homework Heist, and I want to talk about it even though Jimmy doesn't. I start in anyway: "I think we need a plan to stop those creeps from picking on you, Jimmy."

"What about you? It's not like nothing happened to you!" Angie points out. "That's sexual assault, Lisa, and I think you should report it."

"Sexual assault? Angie, you're such a drama queen! Nothing really happened, other than, well, Tyler Robinson being his usual asshole self."

"I'm not so sure about that," Angie shakes her head. A lock of dark hair with a crimson highlight escapes the sparkling clip behind her ear and she tucks it back in.

"Really. It was just a case of me being in the wrong place at the wrong time. It's Jimmy that has to deal with this all the time."

Jimmy says, "I don't think there's anything I can do."

Angie digs through her backpack and pulls out a sort of organizer slash wallet she got for Christmas. It has her phone, driver's license, a few other things, plus a debit card and a credit card, in it. I've mentioned her mother lets her use the car all the time, and that she has a credit card so she can put gas in it, but she's also allowed to use it to buy other stuff. I know it's not nice being jealous, but I am, and I wish my parents would give me a credit card. I hardly ever shop and when I do, I use my debit card. Mom is pretty good about transferring extra money into my account when I need something, like clothes for school, as long as I don't squander it, so I suppose there's no point. Problem is, I always have to ask her to do it, and if I want something more expensive than how much money is in the account, which hasn't happened but you have to think ahead, I'm screwed. This wouldn't be a problem if it was a credit card.

Anyway. Angie folds the wallet open to where there's a little notebook, and says, "Let's start with a list of ideas for Jimmy's problem first."

Over the course of the next while, Angie writes down every idea we come up with, whether we all agree with it or not:

- Need to move Jimmy's locker into one of the main halls
- How to move Jimmy's locker
- Have Jimmy give up his homework without resistance
- What about his own assignments then? Possibly make two sets.
- Make one good set, a second for the bullies that is ALL WRONG!
- Maybe vandalize Jimmy's locker so he has to get a new one? Break hinges somehow maybe?
- Lisa /Angie go with Jimmy when he goes to his locker
- Transfer to a different school
- Take glasses off before going to locker
- Put rat poison in a bait sandwich.

Damaging school property is out of the question, really, even if we could figure out how to do it. The hinges seem sturdy. Nothing short of a big hammer seems likely to work. That couldn't fail to attract attention. Imagine the trouble we'd be in!

Changing schools isn't an option this close to year end. Jimmy says his mother wouldn't agree anyway. He hasn't told her what's going on and says he won't, because she'd just tell him to suck it up. Off the list.

Obviously, Angie and I can't go with Jimmy every time he goes to his locker because it's always when we need to be at ours. Off the list.

Taking his glasses off to protect them against breakage is also a non-starter, since he can barely see without them. Doesn't matter anyway, Jimmy points out, as they're already broken in so many places, what's one more? Unless they come up with a way to smash the plastic lenses, he can just add tape and glue. That one comes off the list, too.

The rat poison idea is something we can only do in our minds, because of course we wouldn't really want anyone to get sick. Well, maybe just a little sick. But it could be worse than just a little sick because none of us knows how much to use. Off the list.

Finally, we decide Jimmy will make two sets of homework, one for himself, the other for Tyler and company. He'll give it up with only token resistance, enough to be believable, but not so much that he gets roughed up. The bullies will get homework that's full of errors, but won't notice, as they haven't a clue what it's all about. The idea is they'll quit stealing homework that gets low marks.

"It'll be a lot of extra work for you, Jimmy, but hopefully they quit before it goes on too long." Angie says, pushing her glasses up. "I don't see how this helps them, anyway, because they need to actually learn this stuff or they'll flunk."

"They won't flunk," I tell her. "They'd be off the team if they did and you know Coach Baker isn't going to let that happen."

"What? Really?" Angie clucks and rubs her forehead. "Hanging with you two, I find out stuff I never even thought about before. It's like I've slipped into a parallel universe."

"Yeah, Fancy Private School to Mediocre Senior Secondary. You must be experiencing culture shock."

"I'm mostly over it I guess. At least I'm starting to think you guys are normal."

"Oh my god, it's too late! You can't get out now!"

"My old school wasn't that different, you know. There was still a hierarchy. I wasn't at the top of the pecking order, believe me."

"That surprises me! You got picked on, like the Lipstick Penis incident?"

"No, much smaller school, there'd be hell to pay if someone scrawled over a locker like that. Post-It Notes was their medium of choice. And, umm, it was more subtle I guess. But everyone felt it. You know what they say, everyone needs someone to look down on. At Queen Ann's, it was more about whose family had the most money. You know, who got picked up in Fords and who got picked up in Range Rovers and Porsches. I still haven't figured out what it's about here."

"I don't know either. I don't know what happened with Nicole and Jarrett, why they're like they are now. I don't think it's me that's changed. Oh, well," I sigh. "Ancient history."

"It really is too bad your locker's so far out of the way, Jimmy," Angie says. "I wonder who dreams up these locker assignments. It's nowhere near your home room even."

"Nowhere near anything, for that matter," I agree, "except the boiler room, maybe."

"It's called the physical plant, and that's in the sub-basement." Jimmy says. Then: "Sorry. Don't mean to be a snotty little know-it-all."

Jimmy and his mansplaining. I say, "It's okay. I like knowing what stuff is called. You know, the right words. Like 'concrete sidewalk' and not 'cement sidewalk'."

Angie looks at each of us with a *who gives a fart?* expression.

"I guess the lockers closer to my home room were already assigned. I didn't start at the beginning of the year. We didn't move here until October."

"Makes sense I suppose," I nod. "Hey, I never asked. Where did you come from? Why did you move here?"

Jimmy turns beet red.

I don't understand how I embarrassed him, but I wish I hadn't asked the questions all the same. "Sorry. Too personal?"

"It's okay," he says quietly, "it's a reasonable question. We lived in Terrace. My dad's in Wilkinson. He wanted us—my mother, anyway— to live closer. Conjugal visits and all."

Jimmy is almost purple at this last bit of information and concentrates on picking at the laminate peeling from the edge of the table.

I can't think of what to say. It's a conversation-stopper. I'm sure anything I'd come up with would make it worse. I leave it to Angie. She's diplomatic. Despite her fine education, she's at a loss for words. This is probably something they didn't cover at Queen Ann's. Finally, Angie says, "I'm sorry, Jimmy. And you don't have to tell us what he's in for unless you want to. Speaking for both of us, it doesn't change what we think of you."

See? It took her a while, but she came up with the right thing. "And it goes without saying," I add, points for me, "this stays between us."

The lunchroom has emptied and it's time to go to our lockers and get organized for the afternoon's classes. Jimmy assures us he doesn't need an escort, since they've already stolen his homework for the day.

# SEVEN

1

FRIDAY AT LUNCH, Jimmy reports having handed over the bait homework after only a minor scuffle. He says, "I wonder. What'll they do when they get lousy grades on those assignments, and I, umm, don't."

"Oh! I guess we didn't think about that." I say.

"Do they have to know what your mark is?" Angie asks. "Nobody broadcasts their marks. I'm sure you don't. They won't ask you, will they?"

Jimmy shrugs.

"I don't think so," I say. "They'll probably assume your mark is the same as theirs. Maybe it's not a problem. Just try and act all disappointed when you get your assignment back, like you got a bad mark, too, and stay under the radar." I'm always happy to give advice. Like he couldn't have thought of that on his own.

"But they still took your lunch?" Trust Angie to notice that. I did mention she's a really nice person. "What? Oh, yeah." Jimmy pulls a library book from his backpack and opens it to a bookmarked page. I slide half my sandwich and a cookie in front of him, wondering why he looks frazzled, and I'm about to ask him if there's something else wrong, when Angie asks, "Has anyone given any more thought to what we might do for the science fair?" And so we carry on talking about that, without coming up with any bright ideas.

As we're leaving the lunchroom, I'm singled out by two boys from my English Lit class. This is puzzling, because they've never been friendly before.

One says "Hi. I'm Liam. In your English Lit class?" He's the taller of the two, but still, the top of his ear is about at my chin. Also, there's this big, ripe zit in the little crease at the side of his nose. I wonder why he hasn't squeezed it. Luckily its location means he probably doesn't realize I'm staring at it instead of looking deep into his eyes.

"Hi, Liam." I say. I'm taken by surprise but even so, I haven't said anything idiotic so far. For instance, I haven't asked him why he hasn't squeezed the zit.

"Hey, what did you think of *The Lottery*? We're supposed to critique that crazy thing?"

"Er. Well. I agree it's dark, but not crazy." We read and discussed it in class this morning. A thirty- to fifty-word critique is the assignment for Monday. I've read it before and I've even read reviews about it, so it'll be a piece of cake for me. I may have blabbed about it in class, just a little, maybe, like I'm a frickin' expert. It doesn't take much since I'm probably the only one in class and maybe in the whole school who reads old stuff like this. Lots of kids have read *Harry Potter* and *The Hobbit*, and maybe even *The Hunger Games*, and *Twilight*, but how many kids bother with *The Lottery* or *Cat's Eye*? I've even read *The Great Gatsby*.

Did you know F. Scott Fitzgerald's wife's name was Zelda? Maybe I should give some thought to changing the Temporary Name I gave Laurie Ann's friend. But then, Zelda Fitzgerald was off-the-wall nuts, taking up ballet at her age, so maybe it's more suitable than I thought. I wonder if Zelda does ballet.

Anyway. Liam and his friend are still beside me and are now looking at me with puzzled expressions. I realize they're expecting more, so I rush on. "Remember, it was written shortly after World War Two and it's satire. It starts off as if it's an ordinary summer day in a small town. You wonder about the pile of rocks ..."

As we pass the staircase, his friend hangs back, leaning against the wall there, while Liam keeps pace with Angie and me. I realize I haven't seen these two in this part of the school before. "Where's your locker, Liam?" I ask.

"Oh, downstairs."

"Well, you're going the wrong way then!" I stop walking. Angie gives a little smile and continues walking.

"I …" Liam begins. "I've seen you in class. I … That is, me and Quinn wondered if maybe … What're you doing after school? Want to hang out?"

"Oh. I … er …" I tell my mouth to quit with the stuttering. He *is* kind of cute despite the zit. Everyone gets zits after all, and he's asking me out! Then I realize Liam's probably not paying much attention to what I'm saying as his eyes are fixed on the front of my sweater. I shift my books so they're in both arms and firmly cover my boobs, then say, "I'm sorry, I have plans. But maybe tonight?"

"No, tonight doesn't work for me," he says. Then he turns and hurries back to his friend, and they disappear down the stairs.

I'm left standing there, baffled. Did I suddenly start glowing like I'm radioactive? It's not like I turned him down. Why the sudden interest, for that matter?

Then I see The Coven coming my way, and I hurry after Angie. She's already got her head in her locker, getting her books for the one class after lunch.

"You won't believe it," I whisper to her, "he asked me out!"

"Of course! Why'd'ja think I left you two alone?" Angie straightens and flips her hair over one shoulder. "You going?"

"Well, no. It's too odd. He asked me to hang out after school. When I said I had plans and suggested maybe tonight instead, he said that doesn't work for him. No reason why it had to be after school. Or why it couldn't be some other time or over the week-end. Does he have a job or something?"

"I don't know, but wouldn't he have said so if he did? I don't think I have classes with him, and with his locker on another floor ... Hmm. But maybe I've seen him in the parking lot. Who does he hang with?"

"Search me. If he has a car, maybe car club? It was out of the blue, anyway, that's for sure. And why not ask you? You're the pretty one! If he's going to ask one of us it should've been you."

"Well, I think you're selling yourself short, but thanks." Angie smiles. "We still going to the game after school?"

"Yup. As long as you're sure The Coven won't think I'm stalking The Team."

"Well, we'd both be stalking them then."

"I wonder if there's a name for girls that hang around basketball players. You know, like groupies for rock stars. Baseball Annies for baseball players. Buckle Bunnies for rodeo cowboys."

"Baseball Annies? Buckle Bunnies? How do you know this stuff?"

"I dunno. Read a lot, I guess."

"Well, find out what it is and that's what we'll start calling ourselves."

"Seriously?"

"Jeez, no! Can't you tell when I'm joking?"

Joking? Angie? This will take some getting used to.

"Anyway," she continues, "let 'em think what they want. Gotta run! See ya!"

## 2

JENNY IS SCHEDULED to be picked up at three on Saturday afternoon. Angie and Jimmy arrive early to make sure she's groomed to perfection. We all want her new owners to have a good first impression. Trust Angie to bring a big pink ribbon to braid into Jenny's fluffy forelock. Once it's tied in a big bow, she says, "There! Now she's gift wrapped!"

Mom brings pop and chips and sets them on the counter above the feed bins. "Gahh!" she says, "have you got a cloth to wipe this?"

I get a towel from the tack room, wet it, and give the counter a wipe. Personally, I think Mom's too fussy. This is a barn, not her kitchen, after all. But I say, "Thanks, Mom. You know, I could've brought this stuff out, and saved you the trip."

"I wanted to give Jenny a good-bye pat anyway. Doesn't she look cute!" She strokes her shoulder for a minute or two, then heads back to the house.

"I could wipe the counter every day," I say once she's out of earshot.

Angie says, "Well, it *is* a barn, after all." Angie and I are totally on the same wave length, even though we haven't been best friends for that long.

I toss Jimmy a bag of potato chips because I know he'd never go ahead and get them himself even though I told him to, and Angie and I take ours to sit with him on the hay. Before long, we see a green truck towing a white trailer coming into the yard. Rick Seville! If I could do back flips, I would!

He pulls up in front of the barn and turns the truck off. Rick Seville steps out into the mild April sunlight, turns and tosses his cowboy hat onto the seat. As if on cue, the sun breaks through the clouds, shining right down on his head like he's in a spotlight. His hair is glowing. He smiles, and if no one else was around I might cry, he's that beautiful.

Angie roots me with her elbow, and hisses, "You didn't tell me he was a Greek god! Introduce me!"

Since I don't know his last name and I'm obviously am not such a social misfit as to introduce him by his Temporary Name, I introduce him to Angie and Jimmy only as Rick.

He smiles and says, "Pleased to meet you," to them, and then to me, he says, "Well, Miss Rogney, you sure look a lot better than the last time I saw you!"

I can't stop the heat from rising to my face. "He saw me with my black eyes and swollen nose," I explain, wondering how he knows my last name when I still haven't heard his.

He stays long enough to visit a bit, give Jenny a good going over, and drink a Coke. That finished, we begin the task of loading Jenny into the trailer. She runs this way and that, backs up and even does a couple of little rears as she tries everything to avoid getting in. Rick is strong, but a donkey is stronger than any human, he says.

Finally, he clips a long rope to her halter and passes it out one of the front windows of the trailer. "Lisa, you come and take this rope. Keep it tight. You'll have to take up the slack as she goes forward. Make sure you're standing back here, so if she pulls, she's pulling against the trailer and not against you. You won't be able to hold her otherwise. Jimmy and I'll help at the back end." He hands me the rope and goes behind Jenny.

"You go on that side, Jimmy. She doesn't kick, does she?"

Jimmy shakes his head. He and Rick join hands just above Jenny's hocks. Not easy when one is about six foot four and the other probably isn't much over five feet. But they manage to give her kind of a lift-push and she hops into the trailer. Rick quickly closes the door behind her.

"Good work, Team!" he says. "She hasn't been trained to go into the trailer, that's all. She's not trying to be difficult. It's scary for her."

If Angie and I both have our eyes glued to him, he either doesn't notice or isn't bothered by it. He's probably used to girls staring at him. He gives us his Crest White Strips ad grin.

There are thumping noises as Jenny moves about inside the trailer. "She'll stop that as soon as the trailer starts moving," Rick says. "But before I go, the people at the rescue asked me to thank you for all you've done and wanted me to ask if any of you are willing to volunteer there. Also, if they might be able to bring other sad cases like Jenny here when they get overcrowded again."

"Absolutely! Yes, to both!" I say in a big rush. I liked having Jenny around, so the idea I'd see more of Rick Seville if he had to haul other rescues to and from here is truly only part of the reason I agreed so quickly. Of course, I'll have to check with my parents, but I can convince them when the time comes.

"I'm in!" Angie giggles. I don't think her reasons are as purely altruistic as mine.

"I live pretty close to the rescue. I can start any time," Jimmy says. "Of course, I'll still help Lisa here!"

"Okay!" Rick opens the driver's door of his truck, pulls out his hat and plunks it on his head. "If you're done here, Jimmy, maybe you want to come with me to Jenny's new home and help me unload her? And then we'll stop by the rescue and get you set up."

"Awesome!" Jimmy exclaims, and he practically runs around to the passenger side of the truck to climb in. Rick slides behind the wheel and pulls his door shut. The engine starts with a diesel rattle, Rick gives us a wave, and pulls away. As the rig negotiates the circle drive Jimmy's small figure is barely visible above the window, but we can see his smile, ear to ear. *Cheshire cat* pops into my mind. I don't know why I never noticed it before. Maybe I should start calling him Cat instead of Short Grain. Not that I ever actually call him that, but you know, just in my head.

We watch till the truck disappears behind the trees, then go back in the barn. "I'm pretty sure Rick can unload Jenny without Jimmy's help," I say. I start putting things away. "I guess he thought Jimmy could use a ride home. Did you see how Jimmy grew about two inches when he asked him — what's so funny?"

Angie's giggling uncontrollably. Tears start running down her face; she flops back on a hay bale, her feet in their muddy two-hundred-dollar Hunter rubber boots waving around. I shrug and shake my head. You might remember how I feel about giggling. Angie is a giggler, not a big giggler, but a giggler just the same, but for some reason, it doesn't bother me too much. Still. This is over the top.

"He's a hunk! OMG! Are you keeping him for yourself? Why didn't you warn me? I would've put makeup on!"

"No, I'm not keeping him for myself. And makeup? For the barn? Is your name Nicole?" That may have come out a bit more sharply than I really wanted it to. I get a sinking feeling and have to admit that if Rick had the two of us to choose between, he'd be stupid not to pick Angie. I don't know why it bothers me. It's not as if either of us would be on his radar, him being probably ten or more years older. "He's gorgeous, I agree, but he's in university. Way out of our league!"

"Not mine! I'm willing to overlook the age difference."

"But he's a *cowboy* for crying out loud! When have you ever looked twice at cowboys?"

"Again, not a deal breaker. And I never said I didn't like cowboys."

"You're crazy," I tell her. But I laugh, grab the last two bags of chips and sit beside her on the bale. As we finish off the chips, we agree Rick Seville was very gentle with little Jenny (very important), Gorgeous, and definitely A Catch no matter what.

"Anyway, you have a boyfriend. That guy who took you to the Valentine's Day Dance?"

"Chad? I don't think three dates makes him my boyfriend! He's a three dressed up as a nine. Not a brain in his head. Why do you think he goes to Western Acres Road Alternate School? But Mom met his mom. She seems to think we must have a lot in common since our fathers are both lawyers. My mom isn't like yours. She doesn't get me. Maybe because she was old enough to be a grandmother when I was born."

"You think because Mom was twenty-five when I was born means she gets me?"

"Well, she mostly seems like she remembers being our age, anyway. You know. Cookies. Chips. Pop."

"Well, yours lets you have her car whenever you want and even gave you a credit card."

"Yeah, I know, I'm not complaining, I'm pretty lucky. She mostly lets me do what I want. That's why it's funny she keeps pushing Chad at me." She giggles again. "You'd think we could go snowboarding, or at least to a movie, but his idea of a good time is for me to sit and watch him and his buddies play Band of Brothers or World of Warcraft or Minecraft or Pig Shit

Land Mines. Cool, eh? Hour after hour. Big fancy house with a view of the ocean and we're in a stinky dark room in the basement. Vomit! Plus, he has a big hairy mole on his neck."

"He could have it removed, couldn't he?"

"My point exactly."

Angie is starting to be a real comedian. I put it down to spending too much time with me.

# EIGHT

1

ON TUESDAY AFTER CLASS, I'm heading for the bus. There's a black Escalade parked at the curb in front of the school. This isn't unusual. I've seen it here a lot. But this time as I come up beside it, the passenger window powers down. I'm surprised to hear my name called. I cautiously approach.

"Yeah, you! Lisa!" the driver says, "come'n talk to me!"

The owner of the voice is alone inside. He has a shaved head and is missing the lobe of his ear. A King Cobra tattoo starts somewhere below his collar and ends at the missing earlobe, as if to have bitten it off. He barks a laugh. "What's with that deer-in-the-headlights look? Just see a fuckin' gremlin?"

No, but I see a snake! If you think I said that out loud, you can forget it, because if he was out of his vehicle, and near me, I'd be quaking in my embroidered boots. I manage to say, "Who? Me?"

"Yeah, you. You wanna go for a ride. Maybe get a Coke?"

"I... er ... How do you know my name?"

"I see a pretty girl, I make it a point to find out her name. And you know what they say, a stranger is just a friend you haven't met!" He chuckles like it's the most brilliant thing anyone's ever said. "Seriously. I'm a friend of a friend. My name's Roy."

"Well, umm, thanks Roy, but, umm, no thanks. I have to study. And I don't go out week nights." Before he can say anything else, I turn away from the Escalade, trot to the bus and in the door. As I head for an empty seat I notice some of the boys watching me. Guys that have never looked at me before. Why now? Is it because I was talking to that so-called friend of a friend?

Next day at lunch, I tell Jimmy and Angie about the Roy Escalade incident. "At least that Liam guy made a pretense of actually talking to me about school stuff! And then, when I got on the bus, some of the guys looked at me funny. I just don't get it."

"Was that the guy in the fancy black SUV with the windows all blacked out?" Angie asks.

"Yeah. Did you see him?"

"No, it came to me in a flash, like I'm psychic."

See what I mean? She's turned into a real comedian.

"Of course I saw him," she continues. "Well, I saw the SUV. I think he must be a friend of Tyler Robinson's. At least, I saw Tyler get out, then the truck pulled away from the curb and cut me off just as I was coming out of the parking lot."

"He did say he was a friend of a friend."

"What was wrong with him? Why didn't you go for a Coke with him?"

"You wouldn't ask if you'd seen him! He's scary looking."

"Don't you want a boyfriend?" Jimmy asks.

"Well, sure, but you know, someone I actually know a little bit, like maybe we're Chem Lab partners or something. Not someone twice my age, as if my parents would allow that anyway! 'Friend of a friend' my ass. If you saw Tyler with him, that explains it, but Tyler's certainly no friend of mine! How would Tyler know him, for that matter?"

Angie giggles. "Well you know what they say, it pays to advertise! I bet the Lipstick Penis incident and the Naked Boobs photo are at the root of this."

"Seriously? That kind of advertising I don't need, and besides, it should've died weeks ago! And why would Tyler bother telling an old guy like that about it?"

"Well what's your explanation?"

133

"I guess I don't have one." I pull two sandwiches out of my lunch bag and hand one to Jimmy. By now Angie and I have realized Jimmy never has anything for lunch, so we take turns making extra for him. We never ask him if he wants it, we just give it to him without saying anything.

"What you need is an actual boyfriend," Angie concludes, "that would put an end to it. If you really want it to stop, that is!" She giggles.

"Of course I want it to stop! It's frickin' embarrassing! But how am I supposed to get a boyfriend? I'm not prime girlfriend material or I'd've had one by now." I take a big bite of my sandwich. It's my all-time, most-favourite, tuna and lettuce on sourdough. I haven't really thought about getting a boyfriend because Rick Seville has been starring in all my fantasies. If you think I'm hoping we'll hook up, you can forget it, because I know there's no chance. At least not until I'm older.

"Well, how about Chad?" Angie suggests. "Or maybe one of his friends? Actually, if I said Chad's my boyfriend, and you're hooked up with one of his friends, we wouldn't even have to go on a date, just drive by the school a few times. We can post some pictures on Instagram. Now and then some status updates on Facebook. End of problem." She grins and tosses her head.

"I'll think about it." I won't really, because of the Rick Seville fantasies and all. But Angie looks so smug, I can't stop myself from saying, "I know how much you're dying to get with Chad again."

She gives me a serious stink eye. I'll have to practice mine, because it's not nearly that good. My go-to move now would be to stick out my tongue, but as I've mostly outgrown that, I carry on: "In the meantime, Jimmy, how's Bait Homework working out?"

He's just taken a bite of the sandwich I gave him. He may come from a rough part of town, but he has enough manners not to talk with his mouth full, so he chews, swallows, and then says, "What is this stuff? Chicken or something?"

"No, silly, it's tuna. Haven't you ever had tuna before?"

"Of course he has, everyone's had tuna before." Angie chides.

"Oh. It's just ... this is the best tuna sandwich I ever had!"

Trust Jimmy to come up with a compliment for a tuna sandwich, although as I mentioned, it *is* my all time, most favourite. "Well thanks, I guess that makes me a great cook, if you call opening a can and mixing in mayo, cooking. The homework?"

"Well, it's only been two assignments so far. Yesterday one of the guys asked me to make copies, so they don't have to. That's how stupid those guys are. Like Mr. Kitson wouldn't notice."

Angie and I both shake our heads, look at Jimmy and chuckle. I say, "You know, it'd be worth doing it, just to see if they're stupid enough to go through with it."

"Naww, really? No one's that stupid." Angie says.

Now it's Jimmy's and my turn to shake our heads, look at Angie and chuckle. "You do know who we're talking about, right?" I ask.

"I see what you mean," Angie concedes. She giggles, then uses a pencil to scratch the scalp under the bun she's put her hair up in today. Spiky ends sticking out add to the effect. It's times like this I regret cutting my hair off, although I don't think I have the hairdressing skills she has.

"Well, I guess you'll have to keep doing the extra copy," I tell Jimmy.

"Yeah," Angie agrees, "but right now, we really have to figure out what we're going to do for the

Science Fair. We only have until Friday! This is so-o-o last minute. I bet all the good ideas are gone!"

"Oh, you mean like the baking soda and vinegar volcano?" I say. "How many of those do we have every year?"

"Really?" Jimmy's snorts. "That's Grade Three stuff!"

"Oh, believe me, it's age appropriate for half the people in this school!" Another giggle from Angie.

"I was wondering ... Does it have to be about chemistry or physics? Could we do something more, like, medical?" Jimmy takes off his glasses and wipes the lenses on his shirt tail, careful not to wobble them too much. There's almost more tape than plastic now. I wonder if his face looks fuller, like he's gaining weight, or is it just that I never see him without his over-sized glasses?

"Like I was thinking," he continues, "how about something about Jenny, what it took to get her better, and the equine rescue."

"Hmm." I shrug and start peeling my banana.

"Why not?" Angie says.

"It would be great exposure for the rescue," Jimmy adds. "I bet most people don't know it exists."

"Well I didn't," I remind them, "and I had a horse! I think Doctor Bennie has photos."

"We could make a chart of the Body Score Index." Jimmy suggests. "Lisa can draw, so she could do sketches of a few of the levels, One, Five and Eight maybe? Too skinny, just right, and too fat? And maybe we could get someone from the rescue, or from Doctor Bennie's clinic, to come for a couple hours."

"Rick Seville!" Angie and I both exclaim like in twin speak, then we both giggle. Yes. I giggle too.

Jimmy looks nonplussed but smiles indulgently and says, "You mean, Rick *Sorensen*?"

For some reason, it strikes me as hilarious; I burst out in fresh giggles, and of course Angie joins in. I can't blame Jimmy for rolling his eyes. It gives me insight into why Nicole gets cranky when I do it to her.

Eventually we agree I'll contact Doctor Bennie to see if he can share any of his photos and records, and if he or Rick could spare some time to attend. Doctor Bennie would be welcome, but I know Angie is hoping as much as I am that Rick will come.

"And on Saturday, we'll all go to the rescue to see when we can start volunteering. Maybe they have an application on line. If so, we can sign up tonight. Jimmy doesn't have a computer at home, so he can do it at my house." Angie says. "Come with me after school, Jimmy. I'll drop you off at home after. Okay?"

"We'll need poster board. I'll call Mom and ask her to pick up a couple sheets on her way home," I offer. "I've got markers and everything."

"I'll see what I can find out on the internet," Angie says, "maybe some good articles, some photos I can print."

"Great! Then we'd just need to put together an outline, a layout, and I think we'll do okay."

"Why did we leave it so late?" Angie wails.

"You're such a drama queen, Angie!" I'd like to seriously get after her but it's impossible when I'm laughing at the woeful expression on her face.

"Well, we have left it pretty late," Jimmy says, "but I think we can still pull it off."

"Plus, we all have to study. Five mid-terms in three days! And now this! Maybe we need to borrow your notes, Jimmy!" Angie says. But of course, being in the top ninety-five percentile of the class, she's not serious.

# 2

WHEN I TEXT TO ASK Mom to pick up poster board, she texts back that she has to get groceries will transfer some money into my account and I can go myself. I'm to meet her at SuperStore. No later than five!

I take the bus as far as the Dollar Store, spend some time shopping, get the poster board, and pick up a few extra embellishments while I'm at it. As I'm on my way to the crosswalk that'll take me to the Super Store parking lot with my roll of poster board under my arm, I see Tyler Robinson drive up and stop for the light. He seems to be the only one in the car. Then a mass of turquoise and black hair pops up beside him. I wonder when Nicole got her hair dyed. With her fair complexion, hair even darker than before doesn't seem like a good choice, but the bright turquoise might be nice. Did I see her today? Must not have. I'm sure I would have noticed.

Tyler swings his right arm around Nicole, pulls her in close, and gives her a deep kiss. I guess it's sweet. But it sure must be uncomfortable sitting on the console. It's not safe, and a traffic violation besides.

# 3

NEXT MORNING, I spend extra time at my locker. I'm waiting for The Coven to show up, hoping Nicole is with them. I really want to see what she looks like with black and turquoise hair. I know it's not nice, but I can't help hoping it makes her look super witchy. But then of course she'd really be a natural fit for The Coven.

When they finally show up, I just stand there gawking. WTF! It's not Nicole who has a new hairdo, it's Zelda. As I mentioned before, her hair is long and black. Now it has bright turquoise streaks.

The girls are buzzing with plans for the spring break next week. Tyler this, Jarrett that and so on. A couple of them are talking about going to California for the week.

Laurie Ann says, "You're so lucky! I wish my parents would let me go!"

Nicole says: "I wouldn't want to go without Tyler, and he has to work."

"He works? News to me," Zelda says. "Where?"

"Dunno for sure," Nicole replies. "You know Roy McDonald? That older friend of Tyler's that comes to the games sometimes? Something he hooked him up with."

"Must be a good job. He sure has a sweet ride!"

"So does Tyler," Nicole says.

At this moment, Laurie Ann notices me watching, and calls out, "What're you looking at?"

I shake my head and turn back to my locker. If I wasn't such a coward, I'd ask Zelda what she was doing with Tyler yesterday.

# 4

AS IT HAPPENS, both Doctor Bennie and Rick Sorensen take the time to attend the Science Fair. The gym is not exactly bustling. You'd think it would be, with a possible extra ten percent on mid-terms on the line. There must be a lot of kids who don't need the marks. There are quite a few interested students, though, and with parents and teachers, it's a decent crowd.

The Jenny Exhibit draws more attention than we expected, probably owing to the poster-size photo of Jenny on the day she went to her forever home. I don't think it can only be because of Rick standing there. Or maybe it is. Even the non-horsey girls are asking him questions, hanging on every word, and there's a surprising amount of giggling, given the serious subject matter.

When the jury, two women and a man, make their evaluations, they are complimentary. Oddly enough, even with the three of us and Doctor Bennie right there, they direct most of their questions to Rick.

Ms. Fisher beams over the project and congratulates "her kids" repeatedly. I'm a bit miffed. Rick spends entirely too much time talking to her, and they stare at each other too long, facts that aren't lost on

Angie, either. She roots me in the ribs with her elbow, and hisses: "I think she's after him!"

"Who could blame her?" I sigh. I've got to learn to stay out of range of Angie's elbows.

Our project gets second prize.

The volcano takes third prize. It was made with peroxide and yeast so it was super foamy, and it was nicely landscaped besides.

An amazing Big Bang Theory project, complete with a dark curtain surround and video, obviously not thrown together in a couple of days, justifiably takes first.

"Lookit that, Jimmy," I tell him, "there's kids in this school even nerdier than you."

"Lucky for the Big Bang team the jury wasn't all women, though," Angie says.

CR☙CR

# NINE

1

ON SUNDAY, ANGIE picks me up and we go together to the Equine Rescue. Jimmy is already there. We've submitted our volunteer applications on line, and Angie and I have our waivers with us, signed by our parents. I printed one for Jimmy and gave it to him at school earlier in the week.

Our assignment is scrubbing out troughs and buckets, filling hay nets and so on. Pretty much what we did when Jenny was at my place, times ten. It's raining, so Angie and I were lucky to get picked for the indoor jobs crew. Jimmy got a paddock-picking assignment so I switched with him, because you remember from the first time he came to my place, he had a coat that wasn't waterproof. I guess that's his only coat. If Tyler Robinson got near it, he could say Eau de Stable and no one could argue.

There aren't many in our group, which is the afternoon shift. There's an older lady and a man who's much smaller than she is but who I guess is her husband. They putz away doing a few things, but mostly they boss everyone else, and four other people our age.

If you think it was just hard, dirty work and we were sorry we signed up for it, you can forget it! It was fun, there was laughter, and we all got to do some grooming and so on. It felt good helping the animals and even better, these kids could turn out to be friends. Angie, Jimmy and I agreed to work extra shifts during the next week, it being spring break, even though the week day helpers are probably all old people. You know, retired.

Would you believe it, in our group, there's even a hot guy? His name's Dwayne Johnson. You probably think it's a Temporary Name, but it's actually the name his parents gave him. He didn't look happy about it and I understand why; it must get annoying, explaining it all the time and no, he wouldn't rather we called him The Rock. (I managed to keep my mouth shut; eventually one of the other girls who's been working at the rescue for a while told us, so I didn't have to ask.)

You might also be wondering how it is I remembered his name, because as you know by now I'm not always good at that, especially if it's a cute guy. I guess it's because Dwayne Johnson is an easy name to remember, even though he doesn't look like The Rock.

He's way smaller, for starters. Well, as tall as me, but you wouldn't be shocked to learn he doesn't go to the gym. But he does have dark brown, nearly black eyes like The Rock. His hair's black, too, and his skin is a nice light brown. No zits or hairy moles, if you're wondering.

Okay, that's a lot about Dwayne Johnson. You're probably thinking I did nothing all afternoon except gawk at him, but you can forget that! He and I were paddock pickers so naturally I was with him a lot of the time, and I could hardly avoid looking at him. That would be rude.

Anyway. To continue, there are ten horses and seven donkeys currently at the rescue. Some are already on the mend and spoken for, while others remind me of what Jenny looked like when I first saw her. One big, bone-rack mare melts my heart. She's got healing sores from harness, scars from old wounds, and is missing an eye.

"She's a draft cross of some kind," the rescue owner, Maddy, tells us. "The meat buyers like these big ones. She's only about ten. Abused and neglected as you can see. Still with a sweet disposition despite it all."

The hours pass quickly and it's three-thirty before I realize it. Rick Sorensen shows up a little ahead of his scheduled four o'clock check in time. He does a quick check of the animals, and then offers Jimmy a ride home. We tell Jimmy to go even though our shift isn't officially over, because it saves Angie going out of her way to take him home later, and we can take care of the rest.

When the night feed chores are done, we're in Angie's Mom's car, ready to leave, when Maddy comes running out of the office waving a paper. Angie powers down her window.

"The little fella, Jimmy, his waiver's not signed," Maddy says.

"Oh. We'll go by his place and drop it off for him. Then he can just bring the signed copy tomorrow."

"Perfect. I wouldn't make a fuss, but it really has to be signed by a parent. These are big animals and they can be unpredictable."

"Understood," Angie says. "No worries, we'll get it done." She powers the window up, and we drive off, heading for Black Diamond Park.

2

IT'S RAINING PRETTY HARD as we drive into a neighbourhood littered with cars up on blocks or just rusting away with weeds growing through broken windows. There are piles of cans and even large appliances discarded haphazardly. Every bus shelter we see is destroyed.

We come to Jimmy's house, deep in the worst of it. Angie's been here before, but this is a first for me.

"This is it?" I ask. "Boy, you weren't kidding. This place is something else!"

Angie pulls to the curb beside an overturned armchair and turns the engine off. The house is set at the back of the lot. The houses on either side have tall hedges that look as though they haven't been trimmed in decades or maybe never and are about to swallow up Jimmy's house. To get to the door you have to go down a weedy, overgrown path.

"I'm not going there alone!" Angie says.

"And I'm not staying in the car alone!"

So we both get out, shut the car doors, and although we don't expect this to take more than a couple of minutes and we'll never be out of sight of the car, Angie presses a button on the remote. The doors lock with a chirp.

There is a sort of veranda, and a darkened doorway. The boards give alarmingly underfoot. I freeze, wondering if I'm about to crash through into the basement, but the floor holds. I can't see a doorbell, so I tap on the door. Lights are on inside and we can hear what sounds like some kind of game show on TV, but no one answers.

I knock again, this time loud enough to be heard over whatever they're watching. Still no one comes to the door, but at least there's a response: "Whaddaya want?"

"We're looking for Jimmy!" I holler, loud enough the neighbours could hear.

There's commotion inside, and after a bit, the door opens halfway. An invisible cloud of city dump, rotting food, and sewage stench even the rain can't wash away wafts out the opening. Backlit in the opening is a short woman so thin and wearing a sleeveless dress so much to big for her it looks like if she was startled, she'd jump right out of it. If she could jump. I wish my brain wouldn't treat me to mental images like that.

Behind her, among the clothes, fast food wrappers, pizza boxes, and broken furniture heaped everywhere, there's a man in just his underwear sprawled on a mattress on the floor. He starts thrashing around and I realize he's struggling to roll onto his back. I don't want to look at him but it's like a train wreck; I can't tear my eyes away. He finally makes it, lets out a belch, then reaches inside his briefs and scratches. If you think right about then I was wishing I'd looked away sooner, High Five to you! You never know what might happen from there, and some things you just can't unsee. Lucky for me, everything that needed to stay inside the briefs, did, at least until after I looked away. Lucky for Angie, she's shorter than I am and was behind me, which means she won't have to unsee any of that.

"Mrs. Rice?" I ask. I swallow a couple of times to try and stop my voice from wobbling. "Is Jimmy here?"

"No." She fidgets and grabs the door jamb at head level as if to steady herself. Then she absently picks at a sore on her forearm before pushing a long strand of red hair with an inch of black/grey roots behind an ear. "That snotty little know-it-all knows better'n to show his weasel face when I got company."

"Oh." I take a step back. Two reasons: one, she looks really mean; and two, her laser breath. Talk about halitosis! You might wonder how I could smell her breath over the stench wafting out of the house. I'm puzzled about that myself. "I'm ... Er ... Jimmy forgot to get this form signed. It's for..."

"I don't give a shit what it's for," she snarls.

"It's important to Jimmy," Angie says.

Like a true friend, she's got my back. I mean, she's literally behind me, as I mentioned earlier. You might think she's hiding, but it's just that she's smaller than I am and I was at the door first.

Mrs. Rice seems startled to hear a voice coming from behind me and leans over as if to see who made it. Seeing Angie satisfies her that I'm not a ventriloquist, I guess. She snarls, "Well it ain't important to me," and starts to close the door.

Angie pushes past me, straight-arms the door to stop Jimmy's mom from closing it, and says, "Well, if you don't sign, you don't get the signing bonus!"

I'm in shock, for two reasons: one, I didn't know there was a signing bonus, and two: I didn't know Angie could move that fast.

Mrs. Rice relaxes and lets the door open further. Behind her, the man on the mattress stirs again and mumbles something. I see Angie's head sort of jerk back as her eyebrows shoot up. This is probably the same reaction I had when I first saw him. She may be wishing she'd stayed behind me.

Mrs. Rice scratches her neck. She seems to have understood him, turns her head and calls out, "No it ain't a pizza. It's some high-falutin' friends of the kid's. They want me to sign somethin'." She turns back to Angie and eyes narrowing, says, "Signing bonus?"

Angie pulls a twenty out of her purse.

Mrs. Rice makes a grab for it.

Angie snaps it back. "You have to sign first," she says, and pushes a pen toward her.

Jimmy's mother smiles, displaying a horror of bad teeth. I realize why I could smell her halitosis. She grabs the pen and signs where Angie indicates, as I hold the form up on the door jamb, then snatches the twenty and slams the door.

"Well," Angie says with a sigh of relief, "that's done!"

"We should've just forged…"

There's a crashing sound, like a thrown bottle smashing on the wall near the door. We bolt, running like our tails are on fire. There's a panicked moment when Angie can't find the right button to push to unlock the doors before we jump in and drive away without doing up our seatbelts and it isn't until we're back on the main thoroughfare under the bright lights either of us breathes easy again.

Angie pulls in to the lot at the first Seven Eleven we come to, parks, and turns the engine off. "Whew!" she says. "I thought it was bad outside!"

"Like Jenny," I say, "I thought I was prepared, but it's worse than I imagined! Poor Jimmy! Wonder where he was tonight? Didn't Rick just drop him off, like maybe an hour ago? Where do you think he goes, you know, when she has company?"

"Can't imagine."

"Damn, girlfriend, you're brave! And you're a genius! She never would've signed without the money."

"Oh yeah? Well, I wasn't brave, just pissed off, and you better believe I was shit scared!"

"I'm pretty sure the two of us could take her, but I really wanted to leave! If that—that *thing* on the mattress had gotten up I would've been outta there even if I had to trample you to get away."

"Wonder what it was that broke against the wall!" Angie's voice is quavery. "I'm glad the door was shut!"

"You gotta wonder what his father is like, if he actually wants conjugal visits with her!"

"Euwww!" Angie gags. "I think I just threw up a little, in my mouth!"

We break out into uncontrolled gut laughter. It helps relieve the tension. I know I feel better. Finally, Angie continues: "I think she sprayed spit on my face."

"Well, whaddaya know, there's an upside to being the tall one! I don't think you have to worry though, I'm sure what she has isn't contagious."

"Who knows what she has?"

"I mean, the sores and the teeth."

"I know that's from drugs, but she could have a ton of other stuff, too." Angie digs a travel-size hand sanitizer out of the console, squirts some into her palm and rubs her hands together. She even uses it on her face. I realize I want some, too, whether or not she sprayed spit on my face, and stick out my hand. We don't stop until the little bottle's empty.

"I wasn't thinking," Angie says. "I don't know why I pushed back against the door."

"You watch many cop shows? Hey, maybe you should go into law enforcement!"

ങ‰ങ

# TEN

1

SPRING BREAK IS OVER and school is back in session. Angie and I are on our way from Algebra to Social Studies when Nicole and Laurie Ann come up beside Angie.

"Hey, Angie!" Laurie Ann says, "hang on."

Angie stops and naturally I do too.

"Is your name Angie?" Laurie Ann asks me.

I start off, but Angie says, "Wait, Lisa."

Laurie Ann glares at me, but I stay put and she continues. "Some of us are going to the river after school. You want to come along?"

"The river? I don't think it's swimming weather yet," Angie says.

"Not to swim, silly," Nicole giggles. "We'll have a bonfire. There'll be guys!" She says "guy-eyes" like it has two syllables.

"One of the guys likes you and wants to meet you," Laurie Ann says. "He's hot, and he has a sweet car!"

"Who?"

"Come tonight and find out!" Laurie Ann grins. "He's *really* hot!"

Angie shrugs and turns to me. "What do you think, Lisa? Want to go?"

"Lisa isn't invited," Laurie Ann snaps. "If you want to be friends with us, you're gonna hafta quit hangin' with her. Also, for your own good, dump that little creep that's always with you, too. Everyone in school thinks it's a total joke, you with the two of them!"

Angie's quiet for a moment. Her nostrils flare and her eyes narrow. "Tell you what," she says, "if that hot guy wants to meet me, he can come to my locker any time. And as for your suggestion about who I should hang with, I'll choose my own friends." Her voice has risen a few decibels and is attracting attention, so she turns and starts away. "Come on, Lisa!"

"Fuckin' bitch!" Nicole shrieks after us. Now everyone in the hall is watching.

Angie stops, turns and calls back: "Did you know genital warts can be spread by oral sex? I'd have that spot on your lip looked at if I were you, Nicole." She smiles sweetly. "Enjoy your five or six more years of high school!" Then she hurries off down the hall, herding me ahead of her.

Just ahead, I see Ms. Fisher has come to the door of her classroom. She gives us a nod, but she's watching Nicole and Laurie Ann.

"I don't know about Laurie Ann," I tell Angie, "but Nicole's not that bad in school. I'm sure she'll graduate with us."

Angie just gives me one of her sort of sideways looks and shakes her head. We're best friends, but she's still not sure when I'm joking.

2

THE EXCHANGE BETWEEN Laurie Ann, Nicole, and Angie is juicy gossip, and it spreads fast. By lunchtime, even Jimmy has heard about it.

"Well," Angie says, pushing her glasses up and rubbing the bridge of her nose. "They just pissed me off and the words were out of my mouth before I realized."

"Well, it was hilarious!"

"I'm not even sure it's true. I don't know if she's got a spot on her lip. Or if you can get genital warts in your mouth, for that matter."

"You can," Jimmy says. "They're caused by the human papillomavirus. There's dozens of different strains. Only a couple cause genital warts."

"So says Doctor James Rice." Angie reaches across the table and gives him a noogie.

"Jeez, Angie, he's not five years old!"

Jimmy just shrugs and with a little grin says, "It's okay."

"Well," I say, "these warts. What do they look like, anyway, just like regular warts? For future reference. In case I do someday get a boyfriend. I'm gonna want to give him a good checking over before we, you know, do it."

Angie giggles and elbows me.

I wonder why I still haven't learned to stay out of range.

JIMMY, ANGIE AND I are all scheduled to work at the rescue Sundays from noon to four. We've become accustomed to the routine, the rescued animals, and the other workers, and Angie and I at least are always giddy at the thought of Rick Sorensen showing up at three-thirty or four. Jimmy likes him too, but I don't think he gets the Funny Feeling I do when he's around. He might, though. I'm not really sure.

You might think just because I said some nice things about Dwayne Johnson I am not as interested in Rick Sorensen as before, but you can forget it. I do daydream about Dwayne Johnson, but only some of the time. Rick Sorensen still gives me that Funny Feeling Big Time, and I know I start blushing just being near him.

On this Sunday, he surprises us by bringing along a friend: Ms. Fisher. Angie and I admit she looks good in jeans and a hoodie. He introduces her to Maddy.

"These guys I already know," she says, indicating me, Angie and Jimmy. "So, this was the inspiration for your science project, eh?"

"Well, yes, although Jenny was at my place, not here." I tell her. "They didn't have room here, she needed daily nursing, and, well, I'd just lost my horse."

She already knows about this, but she still gets that soft look in her eyes when I bring it up. I suddenly realize how much having Jenny depending on me helped me get over losing Wembly. I'm going to have to thank Doctor Bennie the next time I see him.

"Well, I don't know anything about horses or donkeys, but I'd like to help," Ms. Fisher is saying. "Rick and I talked about organizing a fundraiser of some sort. We thought about something at the school"

If you think I get a sinking feeling when I hear about her and Rick Sorensen discussing fund raisers, which obviously means today isn't the first time they've been together, a not very happy High Five for you.

"That would be great," Maddy says. "We need so much. Stuff people wouldn't even think of. Right down to fence posts and nails!"

"You three," she indicates Lisa, Angie and Jimmy, "can you come to my classroom tomorrow, twelve thirty? We'll start working out a plan." Her slightly lopsided smile shows her left upper canine protruding just a little bit. I'd like to say it spoils her looks but have to admit it doesn't. Rick obviously doesn't think so, either, because he's looking at her as if she's The Sun and The Moon and as they leave, he takes her hand.

"Aww, damn!" Angie moans when they're out of earshot, "By the time I'm out of high school, the good ones will all be taken."

"Don't be stupid! You're for sure going to university and you'll have dozens of guys after you! Surprised you don't already." I move a few steps away so I'm out of elbow range, just in case.

"She's too good looking," Jimmy says. "Guys are afraid to ask her out."

"Oh, the oracle has spoken!" Angie says, but she laughs and ruffles his hair. "Thanks, anyway. Looks like you need a ride home, eh?"

ೞഏೞ

# ELEVEN

## 1

ON MONDAY, JIMMY isn't at school. Angie and I go to see Ms. Fisher at lunch time anyway, and we have an abbreviated first fundraiser meeting, just getting down some ideas. The school book sale was a flop. She says that towards the end of it, they were begging people to take books, five for a dollar even. I wish I could have stayed longer! But the cookies sold well. It wouldn't do as a fundraiser for the Rescue as a stand-alone thing, but maybe an open house with a cookie table at that. Also maybe a raffle? Who's going to solicit prizes? And so on.

When Jimmy doesn't show up on Tuesday, either, I start to think something's wrong.

"We should go and see him," Angie says.

"Are you kidding? After the Waiver Signing Incident?"

"I know! I don't look forward to it, believe me. But he never misses school. There must be something wrong."

"We could phone," Lisa suggests.

"Sure, if Jimmy had a phone! Do you think there's a landline in that dump?"

"You never know. Let's see if there's a listing." There's one Rice, but not on Jimmy's street.

"We can't just do nothing," I say.

"Of course not! Someone needs to go there, but maybe instead of us, it should be someone scarier than us."

"Well, at least bigger and more official."

"Who?"

"Maybe the principal?" I suggest. "He could just phone, even. They must have a phone number for his mom, like her cell number or maybe an unlisted number, in the office. Can we talk to Ms. Fisher about it? *Should* we talk to her about it?"

"Yes, we should."

We go to her classroom and hang around like a bad smell, waiting for the period to end. Finally the bell rings, the door bumps open and the students pour out. She's calling out assignments as they leave.

"Huh! She does that to everyone," I remark. Angie and I push in past the exiting students.

Ms. Fisher looks up, surprised to see us. I say, "Ms. Fisher, sorry to barge in, but we really need to talk to you."

When Mrs. Fisher hears the start of the story, she asks Angie to go and lock the rear door, while she gets up and goes to the front door. She tells students on their way in to wait while she deals with an important issue, then closes and locks that door.

It's not as short a story as we thought it would be. Before I know it, I'm jabbering away about Jimmy's mom and the scabby sores she was picking at and her awful teeth and the Creature from the Black Lagoon flopping around on the mattress in his underwear. You know, a bunch of stuff that has nothing to do with anything. I don't even leave out the part where his mother called him a snotty little know-it-all and said that he knows better than to show his little weasel face when she has company. I think she needs to know everything we do to understand why we're concerned. I'm surprised Ms. Fisher lets me run off at the mouth like that, but then, Angie's chiming in so it isn't just one hysterical teenager with an over-active imagination. If I haven't said so before, I can count on Angie to have my back.

"Well," Ms. Fisher says when we finally run out of steam, "this is a lot to digest. I'll have to give it some thought. As a starting point, I'll send the School Board's psychologist to the Rice address, today, for sure. And I will have Jimmy's locker assignment changed immediately." She paces around her desk, arms akimbo. "That's the easy stuff. The hard stuff will be proving who's been assaulting him all these months."

"I'll be a witness!" I volunteer so quickly you might think I'm really confident and brave. I find it's easy to take on something that's off in the future, for two reasons: one, if it's a long ways off, you have plenty of time to prepare yourself; and two, you never know, anything can happen in the meantime and you might end up not having to do anything but you'll still get points for volunteering.

You shouldn't think it's a hollow promise in this case, though, because I totally would testify against them if it came to that. If testify is the right word for ratting out someone to the school principal.

"Yes, but I'd rather not get you into it, at least not if we don't have to. You still have to show up here every day, after all."

"Is there any way of comparing the answers on the chemistry assignments? I mean, would you need a warrant or anything for that? Can you go just by the marks, which would be school records?"

"We might need their parents' permission." Ms. Fisher slides into a student desk near the two girls and drums her fingers on the desktop. I forget about Jimmy for a couple of seconds when I notice she's got chewed nails and you can call me mean and spiteful if you want, but I'm kind of glad to see she's got a bad habit. I mean, nail chewing, lopsided smile and an eye tooth that sticks out a little too far? She's not as perfect as I always thought and look how great she is. Which means there's hope for people who aren't perfect, and when you think about it, that's everyone.

"Hey!" Angie exclaims. "What if we had the chemistry teacher make up a special assignment for just one class ... Is there one with just Ethan ... Tyler ... what's that other guy's name again? With one question that hasn't got an answer in the book. Have him give Jimmy the answer."

"I see where you're going with that, Angie," I know I'm interrupting her train of thought and she probably has a really good plan cooking away there, but I am so worried about Jimmy my insides are starting to quake. I guess telling Ms. Fisher all those details brought it all up. "But right now I really just need to know Jimmy's okay. I can't concentrate on anything else."

"You know, I'm going to talk to the cop." Ms. Fisher says. "I think she's supposed to be here this afternoon."

"But what about Jimmy?"

"Give me your cell numbers and I'll call you as soon as I know something. Go on! Let me get after this."

"But someone will look for him today? Absolutely?"

"Yes, today. Even if I have to go myself."

Shortly after we leave, the assistant principal passes us in the hall, heading for Ms. Fisher's classroom. Then, there's a flurry of movement and chatter as Ms. Fisher's entire third period Biology class gets an unexpected spare and wends its way to the library.

With our worry over Jimmy, neither Angie nor I pay attention to the goings on in The Coven. I barely even give a thought to Nicole not being with them, although I do think it's odd when I see her skulking along the hall by herself. She looks funny, too, all puffy around her eyes. I just think that either she's got a big allergic reaction to all that make-up she's been slathering on lately or she's been crying. By now I'm used to her completely ignoring me so if I have any thoughts about asking her what's wrong, I forget about it. I don't hear the news until sixth period.

Tyler dumped her.

## 2

LATER THAT NIGHT, I'm tossing and turning, unable to fall asleep. It's not surprising, since I've been in such a dither all day. My cell rings. It's Ms. Fisher, and she tells me Jimmy has been apprehended by Social Services.

"Oh! Well, that's great, isn't it?" I say, but Ms. Fisher doesn't sound like she thinks it's such a good thing.

"Well, it would be, and probably will be, except right now he's in the hospital."

"In the hospital? Why? What's wrong?"

"He's hurt. He was beaten up."

"Oh my god!" I jump out of bed, unsure what to do. Would Mom take me to the hospital to see him? Should I wait until morning? Should I go at all? I ask, "Should I go see him?"

"Not tonight. He'll be asleep now. I only called you because I said I would as soon as I knew something, and I know you were worried. Come to school tomorrow. Check in at the office, Mr. Dvorak is in the loop and wants to meet with you, too. And if Angie doesn't have her mom's car, I'll drive you over to the hospital at lunch time. Okay?"

"Okay."

"I'll call Angie now."

I've barely hung up when there's a tap on my door and Mom sticks her head in. "I heard your phone. It's awfully late for someone to be calling. Who was it?"

"Oh Mom, it was Ms. Fisher! Jimmy's been beaten up and he's in the hospital."

"Oh my god! How? What happened?"

"That's all I know." I struggle to hold back tears. "Ms. Fisher's going to tell us more tomorrow. Oh Mom!" Now I start yodeling. I can't hold it back. "You should see how awful his mother is! And his house ... his mother is covered with sores and scratches at herself ... her teeth! Agghh! I can't even *describe* how horrible she is! And the Creature from the Black Lagoon! The awful man!" I flop down on my bed, put my face in my hands, and start going at it big time.

Mom sits beside me and pulls me into a hug. "Okay ... okay ... okay."

"Social Services apprehended him!" I manage to squawk out between sobs. I reach for a Kleenex off the night table, and honk into it. "Surely he won't have to go back there to that awful place! It's bad enough he gets picked on all the time at school and he's not even safe at home!"

"Lisa," Mom says, "let's go downstairs and make tea. Dad needs to hear this. And you're going to tell us how you know all this."

3

NORMALLY I SLEEP like a dead person but I was so worked up about Jimmy, I just tossed and turned all night. Well, not quite all night. I fell asleep about two, shortly after Big Mutt jumped up on my bed. You might think having a hundred-and-something pound fur ball on your bed would make it hard to sleep but you can forget it. Two reasons: one, if Big Mutt wants to snuggle you, you will be snuggled, which puts an end to the tossing and turning; and two, I have the queen-sized bed I got handed down from Mom and Dad when they got their new king-sized one, so there is room for both of us. Unless of course Big Mutt decides to sleep crosswise. Then I just cling to the edge of the bed and hope he doesn't stretch out his feet and push me off. He didn't; I slept, and I woke up before my alarm went off at six.

You might wonder why anyone would wake up before their alarm if they'd had such a hard time falling asleep. I normally hit the snooze button at least twice, even when I have slept like a dead person. But if you have a dog, you probably know that for some reason, a dog just quietly staring at you six inches from your face can be more effective than an alarm clock, even if their breath doesn't smell like they've been eating horse poop. Should you be lucky enough to sleep through the staring until the licking starts, you won't be able to sleep through that.

Big Mutt goes out to do his business every morning at six and he is a creature of habit. To solve this problem, Dad installed a doggie door. Because he's as big as a person, the doggie door is big enough for a person too, so it's in the garage. You might think that's an odd place for it, but we wouldn't want just anything, you know, like Big Mutt when he's been in the mud, or other dogs, or rats, or robbers, using it. This means we have to remember to leave the door into the garage open when we go to bed. I'm guessing in all the fuss last night, we didn't, and if you have a dog the size of Big Mutt, you are not going to ignore him when he lets you know he needs to go out because of consequences I'm sure you can imagine.

It's also worth mentioning here that Big Mutt is not a guard dog, in case you were wondering about him letting robbers in. The sight of this giant dog should be enough to keep robbers away, but if a robber got close enough to see Big Mutt with his big grin, the only thing a robber would have to worry about would be getting licked to death which would be bad enough even if he hadn't been eating horse poop.

Anyway. I was up early, got dressed in a hurry, and was ready an hour and a half before it was time for us to go. I decide to start drinking coffee because from what I've seen, that's what a lot of people do when they have time to kill. If you think I haven't tried it before, you can forget it because I have, more than once. Each time, I figured it must be something you have to learn to love or there was some other secret to it. This morning I try adding lots of Mom's Cinnabon. Secret revealed! I have two cups.

You may have noticed I said, "time for us to go", not "time for me to go". This is because Mom and Dad are going with me. I'm glad about that for two reasons: one, it saves me having to ride on the bus, which if I haven't mentioned it before, can be a trial because it's full of juvenile delinquents; and two, I'm glad to have them with me because I don't know what to expect from the meeting with Principal Dvorak. I hope he hasn't done a background check on me and found the forged notes in the Lisa Rogney's Life in High School file. I push that worry out of my mind. What's the worst they can do? I don't have my driver's licence yet. Anyway, the big concern is Jimmy, beaten up and lying in a hospital bed, and I must be a very small person to be worrying about being grounded, car or no car.

# 4

WE CHECK IN at the office and find out because there are so many people, the meeting is in the teacher's lounge.

Present are me and my parents, and Angie and hers. (It's nice they meet each other. Maybe we can become Family Friends! Although her parents are a lot older and look like grandparents.)

Ms. Fisher and the school principal, Mr. Dvorak.

The School Board's psychologist, Doctor Milott and a social worker from Child Protection Services, Ms. Lawson (call me Jenny).

The school cop, Constable Deakin, and another cop, Sergeant Smith.

The meeting begins with Sergeant Smith saying his department got involved when Doctor Milott thought Ms. Lawson should accompany him, and Constable Deakin thought they might need back-up.

"A tweaking addict can be unpredictable and violent," Constable Deakin explains.

Then Ms. Fisher says, "Jimmy will be all right, but he's in traction for his broken leg, so he will be hospitalized for some time. He also got broken ribs and a broken wrist. So he's quite a mess at the moment."

"But the worst news is the evidence of healed breaks in numerous other bones." Jenny puts in. "Chronic physical abuse."

"Mrs. Rice is an addict, probably crystal meth." Constable Deakin says. "At first she told us she was the only one there. Hadn't seen Jimmy because he'd moved out."

Jenny chimes in again: "That's when I told her if he'd moved out, her welfare would be cut back."

"Yeah," Sergeant Smith picks up the story. "Then she claimed he was with friends and would home be in a day or two. Ms. Lawson insisted on seeing his room as proof he hadn't moved out, or she wouldn't have let us in. We would've needed a warrant. So it was lucky."

"Jimmy's room is marginal," Jenny says and shakes her head with a *tsk*. "His back pack was there, though. We didn't think he'd go away and leave that behind."

Between the police officers and the social worker, the rest of the story unfolds. Jimmy was on a mattress in a semi-basement area under the house. It appeared he'd spent a lot of time there. A low door allowed access to the alley, but there was also a trap door to the main part of the house. His attacker likely dropped him through the trap door.

"Of course, Mrs. Rice knows nothing about it. Her story is that someone must have broken in and beaten him up when she wasn't home," Sergeant Smith says. "I understand you girls were at the house a week or two before and saw a man there then. Do you think you could describe him?"

"I was behind Lisa so I didn't get a good look at him," Angie says.

"You were the lucky one!" I tell Angie. Then to everyone else: "I saw him, but really, I tried not to look at him! Especially when he started scratching, you know, his ... you know. But maybe if I could look at some photos?"

"We'll be talking to Jimmy," Sergeant Smith says. "Hopefully he can tell us who did it."

"There's also the matter of that assault on Jimmy here at the school," Constable Deakin says. "I wish you kids had reported it to me when it happened."

I see Angie's giving me one of her looks, so she is totally jamming out. I stare at my feet for a moment before saying, "We thought we could deal with it ourselves. And Jimmy didn't want to report it. He thought it would just make it worse. Bad enough at school, but he gets beaten up at home, too! Poor Jimmy."

I feel my lower lip starting to tremble, so I clamp onto it with my teeth. I really don't want to start yodeling in front of all these people. I can't stop my eyes from filling with tears, though.

"Lisa," Constable Deakin says, "You know most kids who get bullied are embarrassed about it. In Jimmy's case, he probably thinks he deserves it. That's why it's so hard to stop! You at least tried to stop those boys. Most kids stand around and watch and do nothing."

"Yeah, that time I did. But back before Christmas they stuffed him in a locker and I was one of those who just watched. There was a bunch of us. Everyone was laughing." I study my hands and mumble, "I laughed, too."

"Oh, Lisa!" Mom says. I can't say for sure, but I think she's not real proud of me at this moment.

"It's really hard to break from the crowd," Ms. Lawson says in what I imagine is a tone they get you to practice at social worker school, "not many do. You likely thought there was no harm in it, he wouldn't be hurt, and it was just a one-time gag. Don't beat yourself up."

"So," Principal Dvorak says, "this wasn't an isolated incident? He's been assaulted before?"

I nod. "I only saw those two times, but he says the same group of boys bothers him a few times a week. He keeps tape and glue in his backpack to fix his glasses."

"Were you aware? Ever have a hint? He's in your class, isn't he?" Mr. Dvorak asks, looking at Ms. Fisher.

"I only found out about it yesterday, but I guess there were clues. I should've paid more attention."

"I'll have a chat with his home room teacher. We'll have a staff meeting. We, as teachers, need to pay attention to those clues and come up with a strategy. We also need to figure out what to do about those boys."

"It's not just those boys, and it's not just Jimmy," Angie says, and looks at me. "Tell them everything, Lisa."

Everyone's gawking at me as if I'm a Japanese fighting fish or something equally interesting. I actually feel like a Japanese fighting fish; you know how small the containers they keep them in are. They can't hide anywhere. I sit quietly, wishing for a hole to swallow me up.

"Go on, Lisa. Tell them," Angie prods, "and don't leave anything out."

I look at Angie, who nods and says, louder this time, "Go on!"

"Okay. Well. Er. I guess it all started when I wanted to tell Jarrett about Wembly."

# 5

ONCE THE MEETING is over, Angie and I are given permission to be absent the rest of the day. We'd have skipped class anyway since we're so anxious to visit Jimmy. We'd have gotten caught for sure since Ms. Fisher hadn't forgotten her promise to drive us to the hospital. She just drops us off and leaves, because she doesn't have the rest of the day off.

We find Jimmy propped up in his hospital bed, splinted leg suspended by means of a pulley system, watching TV. He has a cast on his wrist, and his face is covered in bruises and butterfly band-aids.

"Hey, Jimmy!" I greet him. "You look worse than I did with my black eyes!"

"I'm not so sure about that!" Angie says with a giggle. I take a step sideways and avoid her elbow.

"Hey you guys! Lookit this!" he shows us the remote control, flips to the guide. "Lookit all the channels! I can't get all of 'em, but I can get lots!" He pushes his freshly-taped glasses up.

"Glad to see you're enjoying yourself," Angie teases.

"Guess what else! The food's great!" He grins and actually chuckles.

"Did you talk to the cops?" Angie asks. "Did you tell them who did this to you?"

"Not yet. I know they're coming, though." The humour slides from Jimmy's face; he puts down the remote and picks at a loose thread on his wrist cast before saying quietly, "I don't know what I can tell them. It was a guy I haven't seen before. My mistake was walking in on them."

Everyone is quiet for a bit, before Angie remembers she's brought him the latest copy of *Law Review* even before her father's read it and gives it to him. "Some heavy reading for you," she tells him, "You never know when a legal question might arise in conversation. Look! This edition has an article called *Everything You Need To Know About Estoppel*. Bet you can't wait to get into that!" She gives him a nuggie. "Sorry. It's the only thing I could grab real quick that I thought you might be interested in."

"Again with the nuggie," I say, and click my tongue. "He's not five years old!"

"It's okay," Jimmy says. "And thanks! I'm interested in law."

"Of course you are," Angie and I say. Lately we seem to have a lot of twin speak.

"Any idea yet how long you have to be in here?" Angie asks.

"Hmmm," is all he says.

Before leaving, Angie and I promise we'll come back the next day after school, with his missed assignments.

# TWELVE

1

A FEW MORNINGS LATER just before the end of home room, there's an announcement on the P.A. system that all students are to remain in their classrooms as the school is in lockdown. This has happened three times since I've been here. Once it was because of something stupid some yahoo posted on his Facebook page about the fame and glory of doing school shootings, and once someone bragged he would get even for some injustice by blowing up the band shell. Maybe the music teacher thought he didn't dingle his triangle at the right moment. Another time, it was such a vague threat they didn't even know which school was targeted, so they locked all the high schools down. It's always turned out that there was no gun and no pipe bomb, just a stupid little creep looking for attention. So likely this is more of the same.

Still, I get a jittery, jiggly feeling in my insides. You never know when one of those dump rats might be able to get a gun or the stuff to actually make a bomb. I can see everyone else is as antsy about it as I am, except of course the kids who are too cool to be rattled. You know the ones I mean. The dummies at the back.

I'm extra nervous because I usually take a bathroom break at the end of second period, and I wonder what I'll do if the lockdown isn't over by then.

Mr. Ziegler tells us there's nothing to be concerned about and we should use the time to study. I'm sure he knows more than he's letting on. He's constantly at the door, checking the hall, but if he sees anything, he doesn't update us. We're not stupid, we can hear the commotion out there, so there isn't much studying going on; we jabber among ourselves and wait for what seems like forever. The class bells keep ringing, so it's at least second period before we finally get a clue. And what a clue!

Two cops with guns, walkie-talkies, badges and so on, come into our classroom. One even has a dog! The one without the dog says, "Laurie Ann Reedy, put your hand up, please."

Laurie Ann instantly turns white but doesn't raise her hand. The cops figure out who she is, though, probably because everyone turns to gawk at her. One cop goes to her, tells her to get up, and handcuffs her!

In the meantime, the dog trots around, sniffing and generally looking like he means business. He's a working dog, but I would say from the look on his face, he enjoys his job. He seems to be zeroing in on the backpacks and ignoring those of us who don't have ours with us, although he does give someone's purse a quick look. Then he stops and sniffs Emily's backpack. So you know what happens after that! The dog gets a little treat, the backpack is searched, and Emily gets handcuffs too. Emily and Laurie Ann are taken out and don't return.

The whole school is buzzing all day. To no one's surprise, Tyler Robinson was one of the kids arrested. I find out Jarrett was arrested, too, but oddly enough, I seem to be the only one surprised about that.

The whole thing is a source of amusement for most people. I guess everyone feels like I do, glad those kids got taken down a notch. Except for Jarrett. You might think I'm glad he's in trouble because of everything, you know, but you can forget it. I guess I still have a soft spot for him, because I can't help but feel bad for him. I blame Laurie Ann. Angie says he's old enough to know better and my sympathy's wasted on him. She's a nice person as I've mentioned. I'm surprised to hear her speak so harshly.

That night, I watch the news with Mom and Dad, at least until the report about the drug raid on the school is over. There were five juveniles and two adults arrested, and a bunch of drugs were seized: Xanax, Ecstasy, Oxycodone, Hydrocodone, other stuff I've never heard of, and even cocaine.

If kids in our school can afford all that stuff, especially the cocaine, they must have bigger allowances than mine. I point this out to my parents and suggest I'm overdue for a raise and that if they don't have sufficient cash flow, a credit card might be the way to go. I haven't seen the two of them laugh together like that for a while. It was touching. When they finally quit laughing, Mom suggested maybe I should look for an after-school job.

Anyway. The drug raid. The adults are both students at the school, and they're the only ones that can be named. If you guessed Tyler Robinson is one of them, High Five for you, because from what I've told you about him so far, you could be excused for thinking he's not an adult. Imagine being nineteen and still in my biology class! I think I mentioned he is a little lacking in the brains department.

Oh! It turns out Zelda's name is Natasha. I think I'll stick with calling her Zelda.

2

ANGIE AND I ARE VISITING Jimmy again. "We had a big talk with Call Me Jenny," I tell him.

This is his third week in hospital, no word yet on when he can leave. He's starting to look better, in my opinion; his face doesn't seem as gaunt and he's not so pasty white. Plus, he's got glasses that don't have tape on them.

"Call Me Jenny?"

"Lisa!" Angie says.

"You're right. It's not a joke," I agree. "Jenny Lawson, the social worker. When we were introduced to her, she said 'Call Me Jenny'. It just makes me laugh, because, well, you know—our Jenny?—so, for clarity, she's Call Me Jenny."

"As if he'd think we were talking to the donkey," Angie says.

I give Angie my best stink eye. She ignores it. "Moving on," I continue, "Call Me Jenny says you can't go home, at least not now. Maybe later, she said. She's going to talk to you about that. For now, she told us she'll put you into the system, and you'll go to a foster home, as soon as she can find one. There is such a shortage of foster homes sometimes kids your age are put up in hotel rooms, believe it or not!"

"A hotel room!" Jimmy says. From the look on his face, you'd think he's considering it and it's not freaking him out. You might even think he's pleased.

"It's not like just for a week or so, you know," Angie says. "It could be for years, until you're out of the system!"

"I bet it would have a bathroom with hot water, and a kitchen!" he says.

Okay, so he does like the idea. I guess if I'd been living at his house, I'd be happy to go to a hotel room. Or anywhere else.

"Oh, before I forget, I have other news, too. Big news!" I say. "I already told Angie, but remember the big mare at the rescue? The one missing an eye? We've been approved to adopt her so she's going to be mine!"

"Oh, that's great!"

"Yup, and besides that, I'm hoping to get a job, McDonalds or maybe Dairy Queen, so I won't have as much time as before. I hope I can count on your help, especially if we get some overflow from the Rescue."

"Oh!" Jimmy says, his over-large eyes lighting up as he grins from ear to ear, "for sure, I'll help!"

"When she says 'overflow from the rescue', she means Dwayne, too," Angie tells him. "He seems to be pretty happy picking her up, so until further notice, it's just you and me in my car."

192

"Oh," Jimmy says, looking at me with a grin, "that's nice, Lisa. Did you check him for genital warts?"

"Hey!" I shout. That kid is getting to be entirely too sassy! I grab the small, hospital-issue box of tissues off his bedside table and throw it at him. The cast on his wrist doesn't stop him from batting it away so it doesn't hit him in his nose, which is where I was aiming. He laughs.

If you're wondering: no, I haven't checked Dwayne for genital warts, but I think I'll soon catch up with Jarrett in the kissing skills department.

3

WHEN ANGIE AND I arrive at Jimmy's hospital room a few days later, we find Rick Sorensen leaning against the window ledge and Ms. Fisher in a chair beside Jimmy. The biology text is open on the cantilevered table in front of Jimmy, and he and Ms. Fisher are going over something together.

"Oh, hi!" Ms. Fisher says as she looks up at us and smiles. "I know you guys agreed to bring him some homework, but I thought I might as well bring the biology assignments. I wanted to pop in anyway."

"That's great!" I say. Naturally I start to blush when I look at Rick and he gives me that big Crest White Strips grin.

"We brought a get well soon gift," Angie says, and plops a gift bag down on the table next to the text book.

Jimmy gives everyone the old Jimmy over-sized-eyes look.

"Go ahead," Angie tells him, "all you gotta do is pull it out of the bag. You can do that even with one arm in a cast."

He reaches his good hand into the bag. Ms. Fisher assists by holding the bottom of the bag. He pulls out a T-shirt.

I can't wait while he fumbles around with it. "Here, let me!" I say, and snatch it away, then hold it up for everyone to see. Stamped on it in large white letters:

## Grade A Rice

"Cool," Rick says.

"Cute, hey? We had it made at the T-shirt shop at the mall," Angie explains. "Lisa figured you'd like white ... I insisted on blue. What do you think?"

"Well, I ... I" Jimmy stutters. "It's just ..."

"Just say thank you," Ms. Fisher says with her slightly asymmetrical smile, "and we can get back to your biology assignment."

"Thank you," he says. "I mean it!"

We tell him he's welcome and take positions around the room, just hanging out while Ms. Fisher gets back into the lesson. Rick and Angie are both totally engrossed in their phones. I listen in on what Ms. Fisher's telling Jimmy, because you'll remember, I'm in the same class. If you think I feel guilty taking advantage of the situation to get extra one-on-one or one-on-two tutoring no one else in the class will get, you can forget it.

"I wonder if the drug bust will change anything," Angie says when the discussion on the chapter quiz seems to have run its course. "I sure hope it's not just going to be business as usual."

"Some people must've been sweating for a while," I say. "Maybe that's all we can hope for."

"I don't know that there's anything to be done about the bullying," Ms. Fisher says, and clicks her tongue. "We, the teaching staff that is, are planning an assembly to raise awareness. Constable Deakin has some ideas for speakers. We want to get the message out that it's everyone's responsibility to intervene, and to report it. When it turns into assault, though, like what they've done to Jimmy and pushing you down, Lisa, it's gone too far. Maybe you should swear out charges."

"I've thought about it," I admit. "I'm not a hundred percent sure it was Nicole who pushed me down, though. I just saw her shoes going by. Anyone else could've done the pushing. Besides, I think Angie fixed her wagon, although she didn't know it at the time, 'cause Tyler dumped her when he thought she might give him genital warts!" We all chuckle. Well, I do, anyway.

"Poor Nicole!" Angie says. "She might have trouble getting a boyfriend for a while, and she's been ousted from The Coven."

"The Coven?" Ms. Fisher says. Then she clicks her tongue and shakes her head. "Oh, never mind."

Angie continues, "But what about Laurie Ann? She's the one who's really the cause of all this."

"How is she still so popular after all this?" I ask.

"I don't think she's totally to blame. Tyler and his friends are a big part of the problem, don't forget," Ms. Fisher says. "But Laurie Ann's a narcissist, and narcissists are very good at gathering followers."

It makes my head ache. I rub my forehead.

Angie snorts. "Nothing we can do about it."

"Well, anyway," I say, "Jimmy won't be going back to school this semester, so we'll just have to wait and see if the bullying continues in the fall. If they try it again, then he'll have to rat those assholes out. Even though they'd likely just get a slap on the wrist anyway."

If Ms. Fisher noticed the swear word that slipped out, she doesn't let on. I guess she's heard worse. She says, "Tyler might get expelled, anyway. Coach Baker doesn't like it, of course. As it is, Tyler's suspended for two weeks and can't play in the finals. Maybe it's all we can do."

"Don't worry, the cops'll get him eventually," Rick says. "I wouldn't be surprised if they're keeping an eye on him. They'd rather have someone higher up. He's just the street-level pusher."

"What about the other two? Ethan and what's-his-name? It's not right! It's not fair!" Angie wails.

"Drama queen," I say. She roots me with that elbow. I still haven't learned to stay out of range.

"No, it's not right, and it's not fair. But do any of you believe in karma? What goes around comes around?" Ms. Fisher asks. "They won't get far in the tournament without their star point guard. So maybe they all pay. It's small satisfaction, and not fair to the good guys on the team, either."

"If there are any good guys on the team! None of them took my side." Lisa says.

"I think you know how hard it is for someone to stand up against the crowd, Lisa."

"I know. I didn't stick up for Jimmy when they shoved him in the locker, either."

"The important thing is, you came around."

"Not until I was an outsider too, though. Angie is really the hero in all this. They asked her to join them. She could've gone along with dumping me, like Jarrett and Nicole did."

"What?" Angie says, "and miss all the drama? Miss meeting the kids at the Rescue, just so I could hang around the mall, or ride around in cars, or go to the river?"

"Everyone just wants to fit in," Rick says. "It's tough being an outsider."

"Until Jarrett and Nicole went over to the Dark Side, I never realized it. I tried to be like them, but I couldn't fit in."

"Jimmy and I are glad you didn't," Angie says, "right, Jimmy?"

He nods. "Right!"

"Anyway," I say, "at least this should be the end of the whole Boob Photo and Lipstick Penis thing. I sure hope no one believes I did either of those things."

"The masses want to believe the worst, Lisa, but that's something you have no control over. It'll die down in time. What I wonder about is whether the police will catch the guy who did this to you, Jimmy," Ms. Fisher says, waving her hand so there's no doubt she means his non-school-related injuries, "if you don't know him."

"Well, we were going to go look at photos, because Sergeant Smith said quite often these addicts have priors, but Jimmy said it was someone that hadn't been there before."

"It's not the same guy who was there when you went," Jimmy confirms. "By the way, I owe you for that."

"Yeah. Twenty bucks! Better quit lollygagging around here, get out and get a job!"

"Hey," Angie says, "it was my twenty bucks!"

"That's right, Jimmy, I was kidding. Why do I care if you pay her back or not?" I take a quick step sideways to move out of elbow range, then shake my head. "So, it's unlikely anyone will be held accountable for practically killing you."

"Doesn't matter. It got me here." Jimmy says. "I just wish my leg, under this cast, didn't itch like a bugger." That Cheshire cat grin is bigger than I've ever seen it. You'd think he just won the lottery.

CR∞CR

# Author's Notes

I hope you enjoyed Wembly. It's quite a departure for me, as my two previous books are thrillers. I was writing The Dark River Secret when Wembly wormed its way into my thoughts. I thought it was just going to be a short story but it kept growing and evolving into its present form, and as I prepared it for publication, Lisa kept whispering to me. Apparently, she's not done with me yet.

If you go to my website, www.gaylesiebert.com, you'll find a sign-up page for my newsletter. I won't fill your inbox, but I will let you know when new titles are available.

If you have a few minutes, I'd love it if you would leave a review. Here are a couple of places where you can do that:

https://www.amazon.com/dp/1981071695
https://www.goodreads.com/book/show/40221817-wembly

91487266R00115

Made in the USA
San Bernardino, CA
25 October 2018